DAEMON'S GARDEN of DREAMS

RAY MARSDON

ISBN: 978-1-7372659-1-7

TABLE of CONTENTS

ACKNOWLEDGEMENTS

With gratitude for Maya who offered her keen insight and meaningful advice with the writing of this book.

Much appreciation also to Pine Island Writers for their helpful critiques.

Special thanks to my sister Sandy, who has been so supportive of my work.

Cover art by Ray Marsdon

"Because it is so unbelievable, the truth often escapes being known."
Heraclitus

DISCLAIMER
Botanicals have a long history of medicinal value, however, those that produce strong mind altering effects can be dangerous, and the author is not an advocate of their use.

Day One

"There was never a genius without a tincture of madness."
Aristotle

"These flowers are making me dizzy," Mara said as her husband Griff unplugged from his phone, and helped her down onto a bench. Passion flower vines, flush with blossoms, shrouded the bushes around them. Large maroon petals and radiant tendrils released a pervasive, tranquilizing scent. A small crowd of people stared silently as their tour guide, Daemon Makarios, stepped over.

"Are you okay?" Daemon asked, his dark brown eyes widened. The morning sun was behind him, casting a shadow over Mara, as he observed her vital signs. His own blood pressure went up a notch, anxious about another incident in his garden. The gold necklace on her upper chest sparkled with the steady rise and fall of her breath. Reassured yet still cautious, he spoke, "If you are not well, you can return to the Sales Center, otherwise please keep up with the group."

Mara took a deep breath from an inhaler. "It's just asthma. I can keep up with your 'little' tour." She wiped the dewiness from around her copper colored bangs, and drank from an insulated bottle. Her green eyes narrowed as she leaned in toward Daemon. "We'll talk afterwards." Although she appeared to have regained control, Daemon detected alcohol on her breath.

Mara and Griff Blackstone recently purchased a home in south Florida, in a newly opened, upscale gated community, El Dorado Village. Bordering their community was this botanical garden they visited today, Elysium Jungle.

Although it was June, an unusual cool front created much welcomed spring-like conditions. The twenty people gathered for the tour moved about effortlessly among lush flowering plants. Most of them consumed the sweet air like an exotic, atmospheric dessert. A few preferred their desserts served more conventionally.

Daemon stood upright, and faced the crowd to continue the tour. Although average height, he appeared taller, elevated with an expansive energy. His olive complexion glowed with a smoldering luminescence. A kaki shirt and pants hung comfortably on his slender, resilient frame. He lifted his hand as he continued, "As I was saying, this is the Morpheus Garden, the garden of dreams and sleep."

Daemon Makarios owned and operated Elysium Jungle. This enterprise, superficially resembling a quaint roadside attraction, actually functioned as an unconventional research center. The entire property spanned 25 acres. The original primary garden used for research took up 20 acres, and was off limits to the public. Today's tour took place on a smaller, one acre version of the initial garden. The visitors walked easily and safely along a concrete pathway, surrounded by a mind opening array of opulent leaves and vibrant flowers.

Griff stood hunched over his phone, holding it parallel to the ground and pointed it in various directions. With his head tilted down, his thinning grey hair was more apparent. Without looking up he spoke to Mara, "The telluric forces are off the chart."

"Just make sure you're recording," said Mara, photographing every plant in her path with her phone. In addition to the broad spectrum of plants, she spied many colorful fungi. There were flamboyant orange chanterelles with their wavy, frilly tops, stunning blue indigo mushrooms, and huge wine caps. Together, they out shown the clusters of ordinary white mushrooms growing among them.

Mara looked up from her phone and asked Daemon, "Why can't I see the actual research garden? That's what I really want."

The crowd turned their heads toward Daemon. Some were unaware of another garden, and looks of curiosity spread among them.

Daemon brushed back his dark wavy bangs and calmly replied, "The pathways are not paved, and form a mix of circles and spirals. It can be disorienting." His body shifted slightly side to side. "It's wildly overgrown, people could get lost or injured."

Among the crowd, some heads nodded in affirmation of Daemon's explanation, perhaps relieved to be where they were.

"Here we have a more tamed down version," he said, yet while being surrounded by vine covered trees whose branches hung heavy with dense clumps of bromeliads and ferns.

7

Mara spoke up. "*This* is tamed down? You're probably breeding all manner of vermin in this garden, not to mention the wilder one." She stared at Daemon and sipped from her stainless steel cannister.

Daemon replied, "There's no vermin."

"Why not?" Mara asked, her viridian eyes contrasting her ruddy complexion.

"Perhaps it's because of the mysterious, exotic nature of this place," he said. Although Daemon knew the reason, he offered a cryptic statement to avoid the reality of the situation, and its potential backlash. The answer he gave did, however, contain an element of truth. Technically, it was due to *exotic nature*; more specifically to an invasive exotic species that inhabited his property, and ranged throughout south Florida. Fortunately for Daemon, these animals remained hidden from the public during the day, but at night hopped through his garden consuming any small creature they could stuff into their mouths. As he contemplated those denizens of the dark, his face relaxed. He embraced all life forms of his garden.

Mara smirked, then returned to her photography, along with the others, recording the exceptional botanicals.

The abundance of flowers attracted countless pollinators. Butterflies stroked the atmosphere with color, like an impressionist artist. Africanized honey bees, potentially dangerous, advanced through the garden with a more visceral frequency. Daemon warned visitors against swatting bees, as it triggered a pheromone release, signaling others to swarm and attack. Sweet or floral perfumes attracted bees, and their use was discouraged.

The visitors looked concerned. They turned and scanned for anything that might be buzzing too close, until regaining a sense of safety, they returned to relative attentiveness.

Daemon moved to a sedative and pain killing plant, the morning glory bush. Its narrow leaved, arm length branches bore purple flowers churning with bees. "In this garden, negative experiences can produce positive results," he said, extending his hand over the active little creatures. "As an example, their stings can heal arthritis."

The group drew closer as he further explained the uniqueness and value of these busy beasts. "Navigation by utilizing magnetism and light frequencies invisible to us is just a part of their daily routine. They eagerly pollinate flowers, arousing and fertilizing the garden." A slight smile stretched across Daemon's face as he observed these tireless helpers. The honey they produced was, for Daemon, life itself in liquid form. His momentary reflection was interrupted by Mara's brash voice.

"Your website states you have 75 bee hives." She squinted her eyes, glinting chartreuse. "Why so many?" Her hands lifted. "It sounds dreadful," she grated. Griff nodded, while still observing his phone.

Some of the members of the group shifted their gaze, or occupied themselves with their phones for a moment.

"Three hives per acre; an industry standard," he replied, trying to maintain his composure.

"Are *killer* bees standard?"

Daemon paused as Mara's words swarmed in his head. "Africanized bees survive better than the European variety. They resist colony collapse and are more productive.*"* His jaw tightened. He looked away and refocused on the plants. "At Elysium, we grow psychotropic plants." Psychotropics affected a person's state of mind. Encompassing a wide range of effects, they included sedatives, stimulants, and psychedelics. "And more specifically", he added, "nootropics, which improve cognitive function." The term derived from the Greek word, nous, referring to mind. He explained that the English language and concepts about life derived from Ancient Greece, such as ecology and pathology.

People in the crowd glanced at each other, someone recalled a movie about a Greek wedding.

Daemon's heritage was Greek, and so he naturally embraced its nomenclature, such as Elysium, meaning heaven on earth. Greek terms also flavored the various zones or sub-gardens within Elysium, like eros and energeia. The extracts produced from the garden were called nectars, and the ancient Greeks considered them drinks of the gods.

"Yeow!" Cried one of the children. A young boy who explored off the walkway, trampled plants as he shook and slapped his body. Small, brick red ants crawled up his legs, stinging him with a fiery venom.

Daemon turned. "If you stayed on the walkway, that wouldn't happen. Hurry and brush them off."

The boy's grandmother brushed his legs with a handkerchief, making sure all the ants were gone. She then knelt down and hugged the whimpering child. "Do you have anything to treat these bites?" she asked.

"You can get something at the Sales Center after we finish the tour. He'll be okay 'till then."

The grandmother frowned. A hush fell over the crowd. A nearby woman reached in her purse and pulled out a tube of ointment for the suffering youngster.

This was not Daemon's idea of a relaxed garden tour. He imagined even the sedative plants were becoming agitated. Softening his voice, he slowed down his movements, and cultivated a calm, steady gaze. "In today's stressed out world, remember the value of relaxation." He noticed that Mara had stopped and was getting left behind. "Please try to keep up with the group," he reminded her.

Breathing through her inhaler, she gave him an icy look. After catching her breath, she rasped, "Rumor has it you never leave this place. Are you a survivalist? Or, maybe you're hiding from something?"

The crowd's gaze turned once again to the belligerent member among them. Some men pressed their hands into their pants pockets, women frowned, and children squirmed.

Daemon's hands clenched. *She's the one who should be hiding.* He managed to once again, project a sense of steadiness. "I do spend most of my time here; why not? It's paradise. And, like this garden, I don't just survive, I thrive." His hands pressed firmly on his hips. "And if I'm hiding, it's in plain sight."

"Yes, *you are* in our sights," Mara said, under her breath. She turned, aimed her phone, and recorded more

11

images of the world around her. Griff followed quietly with his phone, recording an invisible world. His app translated the geo-magnetic forces into graphs, measuring direction and intensity.

Moving more deeply into the dream garden, Daemon swept his hand toward a grove of small trees, as if introducing a special guest. "Behold the angel's trumpet."

Several species of angel's trumpet tree were grown here, and they could be distinguished by their flower color; white, yellow, or pink. The trumpet shaped flowers grew to a huge size, some as long as your forearm. They hung upside down, typical for the genus Brugmansia, as if communicating with the underworld. Facing downward, the flowers opened and flared out into five filaments, some curved upward like slender little horns.

"Look at all the bees," said one of the children, who pointed at swarms drifting around the flowers. A low frequency buzz indicated their wings pulsed as slowly as possible while managing to stay airborne. Many bees crawled or clung motionless on the flowers.

"These flowers release an intense fragrance only at night. In the early morning the scent lingers, mesmerizing the honeybees," Daemon explained. "Some bees remain day and night with the flowers, refusing to return to their hive." Daemon gently brushed his hand across the fuzzy creatures. Out of character for Africanized bees, they barely moved, and just continued to hum. "Researchers consider angel's trumpets the most powerful among psychedelic plants because they affect the part of mind that distinguishes reality from fantasy. This results in bizarre thought and behavior, including hallucinations that appear completely real and solid. That influence can persist for days or even weeks after it's been ingested."

"If those plants are so mind altering, why do you even have them?" Mara asked.

Daemon's face tightened. *I'd like to alter her mind.* He regrouped and responded. "Although they are not used in the nectars, they do offer insight into our research." Daemon shrugged his shoulders, and continued the tour. The visitors snaked their way through the tangled nootropic gardens, investigating plants that stirred desire as well as those that stabilized emotions and thought. They observed an ecosystem that produced and mirrored the chemistry of their own nervous systems. This strange similarity evoked a sense of looking both outward and inward.

Mara, engrossed in her photography, offered Daemon a temporary reprieve. Griff wandered from the group occasionally, lost in his virtual world. The crowd slinked through this botanical mind scape, focused and present as if embodying the effects of the nootropics growing around them. As the tour concluded, Mara and Griff approached Daemon. "Let's talk in the Sales Center," Mara said, " I need some AC."

At the Sales Center, Daemon, Mara, and Griff sat in a small office that doubled as a break room. Cooling off, Mara fluffed her hair, which appeared more rusty colored under the greenish fluorescent lighting. She informed Daemon that she was president of the board of directors at El Dorado Village, and reminded him of several unresolved complaints that her community had lodged against Elysium Jungle.

"I'm not ignoring you, there's so much to consider," Daemon said. He thought it unusual that a person like Mara actually attended his tour, yet he was not surprised that someone of her demeanor held a high position within that elitist group.

"If you want to continue to enjoy the patronage from El Dorado Village, as well as avoid certain repercussions from code enforcement, I suggest you meet with the general manager and myself tomorrow morning," Mara insisted.

Daemon reluctantly agreed. They stepped out of the office and into the retail area of the Sales Center.

Griff proceeded to the check-out counter. "I would like all of your Eros and Energeia Nectars," he said to the cashier. "And some of the other nectars as well." His head and neck jutted somewhat forward, compensating for his permanently hunched shoulders.

"Sounds like you know how to have a good time," said Shavonda as her ebony complexion glowed with amusement. She gathered and boxed several dozen of the two ounce bottles.

"They're not for me, I'm giving them as gifts," Griff replied.

"Good idea," she said as she brushed back her dreadlocks, "spread the love." After ringing him up, she made sure he was okay with the large, heavy package. Shavonda Davis managed the Sales Center when they were open on Saturdays, otherwise she worked in the lab.

Mara offered Daemon a parting thought, "Remember, character is what you are in the dark." And with that, she and Griff exited.

A young woman approached Daemon as Shavonda moved to the office to take a phone call.

"Mr. Makarios, I'd like to have a word with you." Her tone was short. "I can see you have a beautiful garden, and you must be a very intelligent man to put all this together," she said, "but the way you treat your guests is upsetting at times; that poor boy with ant bites, and the woman with breathing problems." She pointed her finger at him. "I would suggest you find compassion for those that are more vulnerable and in need. That's all I have to say." She turned and propelled herself out the door.

Shavonda returned from the office. "What did she want?"

"Nothing important," said Daemon, as he questioned the value and reasoning behind why he did the tours at all. *This method of promotion is getting ridiculous.* He shrugged and looked out the window as the woman hastened toward the parking area. "The villagers are beyond restless," Daemon sighed, as he stepped outside.

He strode past the tour garden where some visitors lingered. As he walked by, dust and leaves began to swirl around him. Trees and bushes rustled and bent. The air whipped up wildly, as if in a blender. His hair pulled in all directions and he folded an arm across his face. Sand and debris stung his skin, as his breath became shallow. His shirt and pants flapped and popped in the gusts. Dirt and debris spiraled higher and faster. Everything spun and blurred. A dust devil enveloped Daemon; by far the largest he had ever seen.

Tornado-like, it twisted itself away from Daemon, and along the tour garden walkway like a turbulent spirit. It roused and agitated the sleep inducing plants. Wind thrashed through bushes, atomizing their medicinal qualities into the air. The leaves rustled faster, heightening to a hiss. The dream garden dispersed into a blusterous nightmare. Trees contorted and wrenched in the whipped up tribulation.

Daemon followed, breathless, staring with his mouth hanging open. It stripped the angel's trumpet trees. Patches of pink and yellow flashed through the column of dirty air. The dust devil turned dark with spores as it vacuumed over clusters of mushrooms. It swirled its way to the edge of his property, over the property line wall, and disappeared into El Dorado Village. Daemon, enthralled by the strong elemental energy, stood still. Chills ran down his arms, and his thoughts circled a still, quite center. He breathed deeply; the wrung out air was clean and vibrant. The storm left a trail of destruction and also a sense of renewal. So dramatic, it must have been a sign, an omen. *But what did it portend?*

A woman treaded softly on the carpet of torn leaves and flowers. "Do you see a hat?" she asked. "That whirlwind thing took my hat."

"One of the most exhilarating natural phenomena I've ever witnessed, and all you can think of is your hat?" said Daemon. His hand pressed into the back of his neck while pondering the uplifting yet chaotic event.

The unpredictable nature of life reminded him of its fragility and preciousness. He quietly turned and walked away. It was time to unwind in a calm, quite place. He headed to see Armando.

Daemon followed a narrow concrete walkway curving between trees and bushes. He stepped over a Florida box turtle whose black shell was overlaid with radiant yellow lines. He appreciated the turtle's ability to consume poisonous mushrooms without any ill effects, and to top it off, lived well over a century. The path led him to a dense cluster of snakewood trees, the source of a tonic drink. He stepped around one of the trees, revealing a door.

Each building at Elysium Jungle was hidden behind vegetation. This created a completely natural look across the landscape; plus, it enabled the property to support the maximum number of botanicals per square foot. He opened the door and escaped into the enclosure.

Daemon's eyes softened as he entered the greenhouse, permeated with diffuse light. Fans hummed, gently circulating and refreshing the air. A spacious room, it measured 50 feet on each side, containing rows of tables blanketed with delicate greenery. Trays of fragile seedlings and more robust rooted cuttings filled most areas. Larger potted plants were grouped together, ready to be replanted in the garden. A lone figure, broad shouldered and stout, meticulously carved out precious new life.

"Armando." Daemon waved. "Taking cuttings?" he asked.

"Yes, we should have plenty," he said, slicing off

four inch sections from an orchid cactus, *Epiphyllum oxypetalum;* a heart stimulant. Setting them on a tray, he allowed about twelve days for the cuts to heal before replanting. Working in the humid air, his light brown skin was wet. He spoke again, "My new crew members have trouble finding their way around in the garden and identifying plants. Can we get signs put up?"

Daemon frowned. "I'd rather keep it as natural and pristine as possible. Maybe you could do some extra training instead?"

"Hmmm, we'll see." He set the cuttings tray aside and asked, "Can I leave early today? It's my wedding anniversary."

Daemon drug his hand behind his neck. "That's understandable, just make sure everything is watered."

"Gracias, I appreciate that." He brought his hands together chest level. "I hope you find someone special. Love is the best nootropic. No?"

Daemon considered Armando's poignant observation with a slight frown, recalling how long it's been since he had been on a date. "A romantic relationship is wonderful, but it's also important to have friends," he said, evading the subject. "Like the drumming circle; I know some good people there."

"They're drumming tonight. Maybe check it out?"

"I'd planned on other things, but maybe." He realized it had been several months since he had been with that group. Extraneous activities like that had to be curtailed he reasoned; the work here was so vital. Yet, at times it didn't feel vital. His shoulders slumped and his body became heavy, settled and stuck in the inertia of his routines. For a moment he questioned what was meaningful in his life. The feeling of emptiness quickly shifted to restlessness, and desiring a change of scenery, he decided to visit Shavonda. "Enjoy your anniversary," he said, as he turned and abruptly left.

Inside the lab, a large counter ran through the center of the main room, adorned with microscopes, centrifuges, and other precision instruments. The cabinet covered walls contained primarily honeys and extracts. Some held petri dishes growing new strains of soil bacteria and fungi. Dehydrators sat alongside racks of desiccated leaves inside the herb drying room. Finally, there was the nectar production area, where ingredients were mixed and bottled, ready for purchase.

"Good day for sales, huh?" Daemon said.

"Too good. That guy wiped us out," said Shavonda, monitoring the production line as the machinery filled bottles with liquid vitality.

"I can always count on you to keep things running." He came in closer.

"Thanks. I like working with the nectars, they're strong medicine. Each bottle seems to have a life of its own," she said, tightening the bottle tops with gloved hands.

"You've become very attuned to them," he said, observing her smooth interaction with the production line.

"They're amazing, I use them all the time." She boxed up a dozen of the newly bottled Energeia Nectar. "What about that other nectar you were working on;

Utopia?"

"There's been progress, but it requires more research. So much needs to be transformed." Daemon's gaze drifted away from Shavonda and out the window.

"What do you mean?" she asked, leaning in with raised eyebrows.

His gaze returned to Shavonda, "We're talking about transcendent intelligence. That's a whole new paradigm of living in truth. It's so extreme, there's a lot of mental resistance to overcome."

"You mean transform the resistance?"

His hands became more expressive as he spoke. "Exactly. Neutralize the fear, anger, sadness, whatever negative emotion or thought is blocking the experience of who we truly are."

"Makes sense. Sounds beautiful."

"Well, actually, it can get messy. Negativity has a life of its own. If threatened, it can retaliate. That's shadow work, the unknown, the unpredictable. It could potentially be dangerous."

"Oh, I had no idea."

"The plant medicines will need to become more novel and more compelling to change that energy. Thankfully, it looks like the garden is going in that direction."

"You know, when I start using a new bottle, I need less than I used to. I thought it was because I was just more aware of the effects. You're saying they're actually getting stronger," she said, filling a box with bottles.

"That's the way Elysium Jungle is designed, to

eventually create not only powerful medicinal effects, but also effects that have never been seen before. In a sense, the garden itself is moving into the unknown. More light, but also more shadow."

The difference between Daemon's garden and his house was like night and day. In contrast to the dense, unbridled jungle, his home exhibited an open, spartan quality. The décor included his prized ancient artifacts; a collection of museum quality Greek vases that adorned his living room. They were a family inheritance, but also functioned as a memorial to his parents who immigrated from Greece, and who had passed from this earth years ago.

For meals, Daemon subsisted almost entirely on what was grown and harvested from his garden. For lunch, he prepared a smoothie. Rummaging through the refrigerator, he chose longevity spinach and lemon myrtle leaves. He added mango and acerola for fruit. Finally, he sweetened it with honey. Plenty of honey. Daemon enjoyed a smoothie every day for lunch. The ingredients varied, except there was always honey.

Daemon sipped the olive colored, lemony sweet blended drink, as he checked his phone and opened up a text. It was a photo of his accountant, Lynette and her attractive niece Cyndra, with the tag line, *see you tomorrow night*. Lynette Taylor advised Daemon on many of his business decisions, and has been an invaluable resource and friend since he began Elysium Jungle eleven years ago.

Recently, she had developed a collaboration between

Elysium Jungle and a local school, Caloosa University. It was a work study program where students received class credits for learning how to grow and prepare medicinal plants. Daemon's guest house would be used for their residence. Lynette positioned her niece as the first student in the initial trial period for this project. Cyndra Faye was scheduled to stay at Elysium Jungle for the next two weeks.

Daemon turned on his computer, and delved into research for his garden, investigating how bees communicate. He listened to recordings of the bees' pulsed buzzing, which they used to indicate flight direction, such as communicating the location of a food source. Always deepening his understanding of life, he spent endless hours with his research.

In addition to exploring the beautiful reality of nature, he also explored the challenging nature of reality, moving into what is often termed conspiracy. He joined a live stream that explored how the globalist's transhuman agenda co-opted ancient Greek ideas of death and transformation. Intrigued by this cabal of elitists, he appreciated their secrecy and tenacity. They sometimes utilized hidden, advanced technology as part of their mind control over the general population. Updates on the latest dismantling of the cabal were also discussed. Corruption was finally being revealed and confronted on a large scale in governments and corporations around the earth. It amazed him that so much of the public was unaware of the evil, manipulative people who were obsessed with control and discord. *They seem so obvious.*

Day Two

"The goal of life is living in agreement with nature."
Zeno of Elea

The sun blazed well above the tree line when Daemon pulled up to his next door neighbor, El Dorado Village. Stopping at the gate, he handed the guard his driver's license, and informed him of the appointment with Jack Landon. The guard verified the information on his computer, and printed out a parking pass. Daemon followed the directions from his GPS as he drove down a long corridor of towering royal palm trees. Although the community opened just half a year ago, they planted many fully grown trees giving the appearance of a mature establishment. What was the cost to purchase and plant just one of those huge palms, much less thousands of them? Hedge rows, neatly trimmed with laser like precision, appeared more artificial than living. Landscapers continuously dug up and replaced beautiful annual flowers, lest the residents became bored. The driveway pavers formed various geometric designs. Daemon actually liked the patterns, although it was an extravagant gesture for a road. This place reminded him of the confining orderliness he had as a child.

It was Daemon's tenth birthday. His mother Krysta drove him through an upscale district in Tampa, with large homes surrounded by well-manicured estates. They traveled to his weekly piano lesson where he suffered under an overbearing instructor. His mother supported this approach, and exerted plenty of heavy handed discipline on Daemon as well. Watching the artificial looking lawns go by, he felt trapped in the rigid structures of a simulated world. As a child, he dreamed of the day when he could freely express his creativity and passion for the natural world.

At the next stop sign, turn right, the GPS commanded. Daemon abruptly journeyed back to the present, and followed the curving road to the administrative building.

Inside a plush office, Daemon sat across from the manager, Jack Landon. Mara Blackstone positioned herself off to the side. Mr. Landon droned on for a few minutes, essentially about the importance of El Dorado Village. Daemon sat in a smooth and supportive leather chair and looked as if he were paying attention. The sizeable mahogany desk between them glistened with a rich, satiny finish. Sunlight sliced through the plantation shutters behind Landon. Artwork of colorful birds and flowers, reinforced the idea of being located in a tropical paradise. Landon's voice grew louder, and Daemon refocused on what he was saying.

"There is concern about the products you're selling, the nectars," he said, adjusting his metal rim glasses. "People are complaining their spouse is too energetic, staying up all night, or others say they are moving in slow motion, with constant naps. There's also nightmares and other complaints… even too much sex."

Daemon maintained his composure in the face of this criticism. "Proper dosage is important," he said looking directly into Landon's eyes, "indiscriminate use is not recommended."

Landon slid his hand down the back of his head, covered with short, grey brown hair. "They are using the recommended dosage," he said, his voice more firm.

Daemon repositioned himself in his chair. "Although the formulations have been the same for some time, it seems the products may be stronger than before. I'll do some testing."

Landon nodded, "Sounds appropriate."

Mara spoke up, "People with asthma complain of the pollen count."

"The summer rains are beginning now. That should help," he said.

"And after summer?" Mara asked.

"We'll take a look at it then and see what needs to be done. Maybe move some plants."

Mr. Landon spoke again, "There is an issue with bees making nests on resident's homes, and people getting stung. I understand that you've already had a lawsuit in this regard."

"That issue has been resolved. We've posted warning signs and are keeping the public well informed and safe. Bees are everywhere, there's a limit to what I can be responsible for."

"The number of incidents here is many times more than the industry standard. The problem originates from your large bee keeping operation, and of all things, using *Africanized* bees."

"People need to learn to live in harmony with nature," Daemon responded.

"Individuals need to learn how to live in harmony with the community," said Landon with a frown.

"This was a quiet, peaceful country community until your corporate village descended on the area," Daemon retorted.

Landon leaned back in his big chair. "You're not the only person who wants to live here in Florida. Millions of people are moving to this state." He glanced at Mara. "We'll probably increase spraying."

Mara spoke, "The final issue is the extreme fragrances from the flowers; residents are getting sick, especially at night."

"They bloom in cycles. Normally the intense periods will be very brief, and then disappear."

"They have been poisoning the air for over a week now, something needs to be done," Mara replied with a frown. "We have standards to live by at El Dorado. A society without standards will eventually collapse," she said, and added, "El Dorado is a huge potential market for you, the population here will eventually be over 5,000. We could promote Elysium Jungle, or condemn it. It's your choice."

"Those plants are vital to my research. I'll get back to you on that point."

"We expect to hear from you by tomorrow. I have a board meeting coming up and I need something definite," Mara said. "Think of these changes as benefiting you also. Sacrifice yourself for great adventure."

On his drive home, Daemon recalled the conversation. The phrases Mara used sounded so familiar. *Sacrifice yourself for adventure*, and yesterday at the Sales Center, *character is what you are in the dark.* After rolling them around in his mind a few times, he realized what it was. Those were phrases that his mother had often used. What was the connection? For the next few minutes, he drove back with his mind preoccupied on the meeting. Arriving at home, it took a moment to adjust from the cultural jet lag.

Wanting to forget the meeting for a while, Daemon opened up his computer. Although eager to watch a video on the elitists' use of psychokinetics, a technology that inserted thoughts into a person's mind, he decided to take a quick look at his email first. He opened a message from Gaia Nootropics, the company that funded his research.

Dear Mr. Makarios,

As you know, our company is being acquired by Psi-Matics Global. The merger is scheduled to be complete in just under two weeks on June 22cd. Along with this merger, our company has done a thorough review of all financials. We have been funding your research for the past seven years. During the first four years you were very prolific, bringing four high quality products to market. You originally promised a fifth formula that you claimed would revolutionize the industry. According to our records, we have not received a viable product from you in the past three years. Due to budget concerns, we will be terminating your funding as of the merger date. However, if you are able to deliver your exceptional recipe by that time, funding will be resumed, provided that it does indeed perform as you had previously outlined.

Daemon froze. He reread it and made sure it said what he thought it said. This could not be. There must have been some kind of mistake. His phone trembled while calling Katashi Nakamura, his primary contact at Gaia. "Utopia is a game changer," Daemon blurted out. "It'll be incredible, but I need more time. It's worth the wait."

"Take it easy, I know what you mean. If it was my decision, you'd be funded for life," said Katashi, "but the people at the top have a different agenda."

"This can't be happening. What can I do? Who can I talk to?"

"Psi-Matics Global is a bit of a mystery, there's so many layers of bureaucracy. Sorry Daemon, I'm afraid there's nothing I can do." There was a brief pause. "Just curious, how has it been going with Utopia Nectar? Any progress?"

"The plants are getting stronger. The nectars I've made in the last couple of weeks are really powerful. I feel like I'm on the verge of a breakthrough; I just need a little more time. They expect me to create the world's most phenomenal mental supplement in just twelve days? They're out of their mind."

"I wish things were different. Here at corporate, we're uncertain about our own employment. It's a tough time for us all."

After hanging up, Daemon stood still for a moment as his blood pressure rose. "Those idiots. What are they thinking?" he yelled. He kicked a chair, and slammed the door as he stormed outside. Pacing through garden pathways, he burned off some adrenaline. After some deep breaths, he returned inside, and dropped on his couch. He reviewed all he had accomplished in the last eleven years. How he created a life time dream, and although some of it had been realized, there was so much more to accomplish. The increasing potency of the garden was a good sign he was on the right track but the details of the mixture, or something about it still eluded him. Maybe he was just kidding himself; maybe Utopia *was* a fantasy. With his mind spinning, he called his financial advisor and confidant.

"Lynette, what am I going to do without Gaia's funding?" Daemon asked, thinking if anyone had an answer, she did. From his inheritance, she guided him to make great progress running Elysium as a business. If left to his own devices, he would have probably spent himself into oblivion.

"Daemon, you've now got El Dorado Village. Also, we've started the online sales again, subbing it out seems to work okay, and there's the new work study program with Caloosa."

"Yes, there are new streams of income, but they don't come close to Gaia's support. You know everything is ridiculously expensive here. The maintenance, the property taxes, the insurance."

"We'll have to create a payment plan and make some cut backs. It eventually happens to all businesses, and it can strengthen your company in the long run."

"I don't have time for that long run. How about

looking into other corporations that could fund my operation?"

"I'll start looking immediately. You have quite an impressive resume, and I'm sure there are plenty of institutions that would support your work."

"I hope so."

"We'll get through this, and just a reminder, Cyndra and I will see you around six tonight. I know you've been through a lot today, if you'd rather cancel preparing dinner tonight, we'll understand."

Daemon thought it would be good to help get his mind off of things for a while. "Keep things as planned. I'll serve a dinner you won't soon forget, and looking forward to meeting Cyndra."

After the call, still pumped with adrenaline, he stepped outside and strode to the Sales Center. It was now closed, quiet and peaceful in contrast to yesterday. Daemon enjoyed sharing the gifts of nature with others, yet recognized the hassles of retail; especially consumable products. He lamented the infrastructure cost, the regulations, and all the aspects of the business side that can complicate sharing his gifts. Is it really worth it? Should he cash it all in and move on to do something else? His life could be so care free. He turned and drifted over to the lab.

Daemon felt a special fondness for the lab. Here he experimented with recipes for various states of mind, and revealed secrets of nature. He considered the endless hours of research here, and although he enjoyed the work, what had happened to the rest of his life? He needed to take a break from his self-imposed heavy work load, and bring balance to his life with more socializing and dating.

Leaving the lab, he meandered through the garden. Twenty acres of incredibly rich ecosystems. Walking the labyrinthian pathways, his pace slowed down. He breathed in the full aromatic spectrum of life, from high floral scents to deep earthy notes. Fiery colors empowered him; canary yellow blooms of tobacco trees, and firebush flower clusters like red-orange botanical sparks. Bird songs, melodic affirmations of life, inspired a more care-free journey. He became more present to his wonderous creation and the Herculean effort that it embodied. Daemon's feet and legs tingled. He bristled with life force evoked by this special place. But it was a place that required tons of rock powders to maintain optimal fertility. A place that needed endless hours of slashing and hacking just to maintain the paths, not to mention all the other up keep. He walked and walked, draining the excess energy from his body. At last, feeling more grounded, he returned home.

Entering his meditation room, he felt more centered. He pulled out a lighter to enhance the vibe with the deep, heavenly scent of sandalwood incense. A beeswax candle lit the room with soothing warmth. Daemon's face softened as a sense of appreciation unfolded. He had already created a version of utopia, a beautiful garden to replenish one's self. The next step, to find the chemical equivalent of that experience. Finding the formula for Utopia Nectar could be just a flash of insight away. There was hope.

Twelve days could be plenty of time. He did his best

to not listen to the critical mind that said this was wishful thinking. His attention settled on the white gold candle flame. Breathing deeply, he savored the sweet, woodsy scented air. The sounds of song birds outside his window created a harmonic spaciousness. Like a deep body of water with a calm surface, Daemon's mind grew very pure and steady. What was most important in his life became crystal clear. No matter how difficult, the pursuit of his dreams made life worthwhile. He knew absolutely the path that must be taken. Sitting tall with fire in his belly, he spoke out loud, "I will create Utopia Nectar, even if I die in the process."

Daemon scrambled to the other side of his house and into his office, conducting a flurry of phone calls and emails, while jotting down notes for his action plan. He called Katashi and outlined a proposal for Gaia's management to facilitate the development of Utopia Nectar. Armando received a request for extra man power on his crew tomorrow, and an order was made for some heavy equipment. Dashing to the lab, he emptied petri dishes of bacteria into a dozen five gallon buckets of water. He prepared for the greatest challenge of his life.

Late in the day, Cyndra and Lynette arrived at Daemon's home. Cyndra stood equal in height with Daemon, who stared at her uncontrollably. Her pale complexion and wispy form, like a sensuous apparition, immediately evoked fascination and yearning within him. Although her blue eyes recalled a bright sky, they also somehow suggested the dark firmament, waiting its turn to dominate in the cycles of day and night.

Daemon's pupils dilated with intrigue.

"Please make yourself at home," he said, smiling. "Dinner is ready."

Daemon sat at the head of the table, and Cyndra and Lynette were on either side of him. Lynette, conservatively outfitted in a pastel blouse and shorts, contrasted with Cyndra, attired in a sleek black dress, quietly scrolling on her phone.

"Cyndra, would you like some rock rose tea?" asked Daemon, lifting a porcelain pot. "It's a Greek medicinal, a super antioxidant."

"Sure," she said as she tucked a blonde lock behind one of her ears. "This is such a wonderful opportunity. I'm so grateful to you both." Her gaze softened as she took a sip. Fragrant steam enveloped her face.

Lynette added, "You deserve the best; Daemon is doing amazing things here."

"Got something interesting there?" Daemon asked Cyndra, who continued to search on her phone.

"Wondering what your place looks like on a map," she said.

"You could see that with a quick slide show of Elysium Jungle," he said as he reached for a remote. On the wall beyond the other end of the table was mounted a wide screen TV. Daemon pressed play, and an aerial view of his main garden appeared. It was a series of concentric circles of land and water. The land was further inscribed with areas of low, average, and higher elevation. Dynamic pathways spiraled toward center and back out again. The arcing canals shimmered.

Cyndra remarked, "It ripples from the center

33

outward, like a pebble dropped into a pool."

"Good analogy," said Daemon. "A wave-like flow of alternating land and water."

Elysium Jungle's complex habitats increased the flow of life energy. Workers in the garden sometimes reported their feet tingling. It sparkled up their legs and throughout their bodies, like the energetic aliveness of several espressos, yet smooth and refreshing like a Chardonnay.

Daemon got up and brought the first course to the table, a flower salad.

"Hope you both like it," Daemon said. "I added a touch of honey lemon glaze."

"It's certainly colorful," Lynette said as she poked her fork through a bowl of blossoms. "Who knew there are so many edible flowers?" She continued to explore with her fork. "It's easy to see how you keep so trim."

"The red ones taste like cinnamon," said Cyndra, with a hint of a smile.

"They're pineapple guava flowers. I was lucky, their season's almost over." Daemon paused for a moment, savoring the subtle flavors. "One thing I like about flower salad is that it goes with everything."

"Oh look, more flowers," said Cyndra, gazing toward the screen. The slide show depicted a pond overflowing with blooms. Their petals reflected a pure heavenly blue, with yellow centers gleaming like the sun.

Daemon spoke, "Blue lotus. Like most plants here, they offer several benefits. Meditation, mood booster, and dream enhancement." He arose and returned to the kitchen, then brought out the main course. The serving dish held baked lotus root with katuk leaves and a few chili peppers on the side.

Cyndra and Lynette politely added the leafy, starchy, fodder-like provisions to their plates.

"The katuk adds a nutty flavor," Daemon said, as he took a large helping.

"It's nutty alright," Cyndra said, chewing on a leaf.

Lynette gave her a hard look.

Cyndra took a bite of the cooked red pepper.

Lynette spoke, "Cyndra, the way you avoid the heat down here, I'm surprised you like that fiery food."

"It's funny, " she said, as her gaze turned toward Daemon, "I don't like it hot outside, but I do like it hot deep inside."

Daemon's appearance transitioned from cool and calm, to somewhat flushed. He imagined Cyndra as a scintillating spice, stimulating his appetite for a dish he had ignored for too long.

After Cyndra and Lynette picked through the main serving, Daemon brought out the finishing touch, a vegan gelatin desert made from climbing fig seeds.

"Do you normally eat like this?" asked Cyndra, "or is this like some kind of initiation?"

Lynette spoke up, "Cyndra, Daemon went to a lot of trouble to prepare this meal." She turned toward Daemon, "I'm sorry, my niece isn't used to such healthy food. It's really an amazing dinner."

After dinner, Lynette wished Cyndra well with her new endeavor and left. Daemon walked Cyndra to her new living quarters. The walkway from Daemon's house to the guest house was lined with night lights, as were all the paved walkways. It was a clear night, and a crescent moon hung low in the sky. Thin and sharp, it hooked their attention.

"I love the moon," Cyndra said, "especially when it's full."

"Looks like you've got almost two weeks before that."

"Well, I'll enjoy the journey."

"Watch your step out here at night," Daemon said, as he pointed toward the ground.

Cyndra froze as a dark, floppy creature about the size of a soup bowl hopped across the walk, then disappeared in the shadows. "Hey, what's that?"

"It's a cane toad. One of Florida's many invasive species, like peacocks and coyotes."

"I've heard of those toads. Aren't they poisonous?"

"That's right, but they also have the potential to heal."

A swarm of small moths and bugs circled around the porch light of the guest house. Daemon and Cyndra scooted inside to prevent the tiny visitors from following them. She introduced her black cat, Nisha, while Daemon kept his distance, being allergic to cats. Nisha's yellow gold eyes locked onto Daemon as she hissed, baring sharp teeth.

"Nisha, that's no way to act," said Cyndra. "That's odd, she's usually more friendly."

"That's okay, she's still beautiful," Daemon said as Nisha got up and scurried into the bedroom. "Just a head's up, if you leave her water bowl outside, the toads will soak in it and make it toxic."

"Thanks, but I keep her indoors."

"Let's sit for a minute," said Daemon, gesturing toward the couch. "Because of my urgent need to focus exclusively on the development of a nectar, your two week training program will be different than originally planned. I'm sorry and I hope you understand."

"It's okay, you need to handle your special project for funding. I'm sure I'll get plenty of useful experience from whatever you need me to do here."

"Great. One other thing is the water filtration system for this house just broke down. It's a rather complicated system, and may take a while to repair. Showers are okay, but I wouldn't drink the tap water. There's plenty of bottled water to use."

"That's fine."

"If you've got everything, I guess I'll call it a night," Daemon said, moving toward the door. "Remember, we're going to get an early start to beat the heat. I'll see you here at seven tomorrow morning."

He exited and walked home, side stepping a few toads along the way. Thoughts of Cyndra multiplied in his mind, like an exotic invasive species. She outcompeted and consumed all other thoughts, changing the delicate balance of his neuro-ecology. Daemon's gate became more effortless as he savored this psycho-food web fantasy. He imagined Cyndra and himself heating up each other's internal ecosystems, like a Florida summer on steroids. He went to bed and dreamed of exploring each other's sensitive niches.

Cyndra was up late in bed on her phone, conversing

with Tammy, a friend of hers back in Indiana.

"What's Daemon like?" Tammy asked.

"He's a good looking guy. Amazing eyes and great hair. He's 30 years old, but I kinda like older men."

"How do you know his age; did you ask him?"

"Of course not, I asked aunt Lynette, she knows everything about him."

"Has he ever been married?"

"No, but he does date women. I could tell by the look in his eyes he's interested."

"Sounds like it's going to be a memorable two weeks."

"We'll see. He's got a lot of extra work to do right now."

"His job may have captured his mind, but I'm sure you could capture his heart."

Day Three

"The roots of education are bitter, but the fruits are sweet."
Aristotle

Velvety grey clouds edged in a searing gold light, outlined the emergence of a new day. Squawks and chirps echoed through Elysium's awakened forest. Framed by heart shaped leaves, crimson morning glory flowers lured a svelte humming bird.

Daemon knocked on the guest house door for Cyndra. A long pause…then the door cracked open.

"Sorry I overslept," said Cyndra, squinting, "had trouble sleeping." She stood clad in only a night gown, with her golden hair twisted in different directions.

Daemon stared at Cyndra's smooth body barely covered with translucent white, silky fabric. "Ahh… it takes a while to settle in." Trying to avoid distraction, he lifted his gaze to meet hers. "Looks like you could use a little boost. Put some clothes on, I'll be back in a few minutes."

Daemon returned, finding Cyndra wearing a T-shirt and shorts. Her black cat yawned, showing off plenty of teeth and a long agile tongue.

"Here, take a couple of droppers of one of my favorite products." He handed her a small bottle with a red label and black lettering; ENERGEIA - STIMULANT NECTAR.

Cyndra squirted it directly on her tongue, then closed her mouth. Her eyelids lowered. "Hmm, a bit sweet and tangy. I like it." She smiled, handing the bottle back to Daemon.

"No, no, you keep it. Just don't overdo it, it's strong stuff." Daemon looked down at Cyndra's hand holding her phone. "Please leave your phone here. I want you to immerse yourself in the natural world as much as possible while you're in this program."

"Are you kidding?" She crossed her arms. "My phone goes with me everywhere."

"It's a distraction, plus it gives off harmful radiation. You can use your phone during lunch breaks, and after five pm, do as you like."

"Seriously? It's hard enough keeping up with everything, even when my phone is with me all day. People will think I'm becoming anti-social."

"Everything and everyone will be there when you get back." Daemon's voice grew stern.

"Okay, whatever." Her lips narrowed as she put her phone on the table. "But I still think it's a dumb idea." She took a deep breath, prepared to go into the world without her electronic lifeline.

Daemon and Cyndra met up with the grounds keepers at the utility shed and storage area. Armando had managed to enlist a few extra helpers for today, as Daemon had requested.

Daemon spoke to the workers. "You are all doing your part to make the world a better place." A few nods appeared among the crowd, some sipped coffee. "We've reached a critical point, there is much to do in very little time. With your commitment, we will succeed. Let's do it."

The workers donned their gloves, adjusted their hats, and finished their coffee. A large delivery truck pulled up right on time, and unloaded a second tractor with a trailer for today's big job.

As the crew readied the equipment, Daemon and Cyndra stood before several large piles of ground up minerals, some weighing a couple of tons. He pulled Cyndra aside to explain the rock powders. Setting his hand on her shoulder, and inadvertently touching her soft hair, it awakened an aliveness within him. Turning toward Cyndra, he asked, "Do you know what we have here?"

"Piles of dirt, um, I mean fertilizer," she said.

"No, not synthetic chemicals," he said, swiping his hand through the air. "What we have here is like magic dust." He scooped up some dark grey granules in his hand. "This is andesite, plenty of paramagnetic and monoatomic elements."

"What does that do?" asked Cyndra, inclining her head.

"It supports our body's electromagnetic field," he said, "and the monoatomic elements open us up to the spiritual realm."

"Okay. I guess it's cool to be spiritual," she said in a nonchalant tone.

He looked more stern. "I'm serious about the effects, it can make a difference in your life."

"Whatever happened to people being more spiritual by praying and doing good stuff?"

"It all goes together; one supports the other," he said, brushing the fine sand off his hands.

Andesite, an igneous mineral, was formed by the molten cauldron of alchemy deep inside the earth. Daemon believed one of its benefits was that it ignited the human energy body, burning away what's not needed in life.

"With this, you can become more you. It supports the essence of who you are."

"Okay, I'll have to think about that." She looked at a brown-grey colored heap. "What about this stuff?" she asked, as she crouched down, then jumped up, and landed on top of the mound. She looked down at Daemon. "How does this support me?"

"Ha, it completely supports you... and the Energeia Nectar helps." Daemon glowed with admiration of Cyndra's agility. With her elevated position, his line of sight was at her pelvis, and her shorts barely covered her sleek legs. He took a deep breath, narrowed his eyes, and remembered what he was talking about. "That's uh, humic and fulvic acid." His heart beat more fully. "It's ahh... a mysterious missing link between living and non-living substances."

"Good, I like mysteries," she said, shifting her hips side to side. Her shoes pressed into the powder, causing little avalanches down the sides of the mound.

Daemon made a conscious effort to redirect his gaze away from the hypnotic sway of her center. Tilting his head higher, he looked into her cerulean eyes. "It's an extremely complex mineral that contains vitamins, amino acids, enzymes, and more."

42

"That's amazing. I didn't know plants needed vitamins."

"Well, some of those nutrients are important to support microorganisms in the soil." His gaze instinctively drew back down to her magnetic center.

Humic acid formed as sedimentary stone at the bottom of shallow seas. Infused with the flowing, nurturing quality of water, it surged nutrients into cells and washed out toxins.

He managed again to lift his gaze into her radiant blue eyes. "You're like the poster child for natural vitality."

"I feel like pure energy." She brushed her hair back, then steadied herself. Engaging the elastic vigor of her legs, she sprang outward, this time onto a mound of black granules. Her shoes crunched down into the gritty pile. "What am I on now?"

He stepped in closer. "Other than the Energeia, you're on Shungite.

She began bouncing up and down. "I feel so weightless."

"It's contagious," he said, watching her youthful anatomy rebounding. "I... ahh... feel a little light headed myself." His body tingled, as he kept refocusing. "Shungite purifies electromagnetic energy."

"Could it make my phone safer to have around?"

"Yes, actually that's one of its uses."

"So, if I carried some Shungite, could I carry my phone?"

"Nice try. It smooths out the phone's frequencies, but not the distraction," he said, wagging his finger, then returned to elucidating earth's treasures. "It's made of carbon, known as the king of elements because of its wide range of expression. As we are carbon based life forms, it helps enable our unlimited potential."

"I do feel unlimited." Cyndra prepared for her final jump, to return to the ground. She crouched down and powerfully sprang up and outward. Underestimating her energized state, however, she almost ploughed into Daemon. To avoid collision, both his hands caught her waist, with one foot stepping back to brace himself.

"You okay?" he said, smiling from the opportunity to have held her, even if for only a moment.

"Yes, thanks." Her face flushed with embarrassment.

Finishing the lesson, Daemon looked over toward the last pile, consisting of a tawny brown color. "This one's not a rock powder; it's ground up cottonseed meal, an excellent source of nitrogen."

"Nitrogen, that's the most essential nutrient."

"Yes, and even though the garden has enough nitrogen, provided by nitrogen fixing bacteria, I wanted more at this time."

"To make the plants grow stronger or faster?"

"No, currently I'm not after the typical uses of nitrogen. Most nootropic compounds contain nitrogen as a base. The more nitrogen, the more mind enhancing compounds the plants can produce." His hand slid back through his hair. "I'm doing everything I can think of to increase the potency of these plants, as quickly as possible."

Cyndra stood with her hands on her hips. "You know, if I had my phone, I could have recorded all that information."

"I guess you're left with recording it with your mind. Remember, we're developing brain power here." His voice grew more serious. "In this place, increasing your discernment and knowledge is more critical than you realize."

Once they were all loaded up, Daemon drove one tractor and Armando the other as they set out to the center of the garden. The tractors traveled at a walking pace, and everyone else followed along on foot.

As Cyndra walked, her head turned side to side, taking in the amazing flora all around her. "It feels like some far-away place, such as the Amazon," she said, her eyes sparkling in the dappled light. "Why didn't you create this garden in the Amazon? That would really be awesome, like out of a novel or a movie."

"It wouldn't be practical," Daemon said. "Here, I can purchase almost any plant in the world and have it delivered to my doorstep. There are very few restrictions to what I grow and do here. It's not like that in other countries."

"Ok, but do you at least visit rainforests in other parts of the world?" she asked. Her voice was speeding up, along with the movement of her arms and legs.

"Keep up that energy level, you'll need it," he said with a smile, and continued, "I did visit Peru and Costa Rica years ago, and it changed my life. But at this point, I'd rather invest my time and energy in bringing the tropical forests here, enjoying them all the time."

"What was your trip to Peru like?" Cyndra asked.

"It's vivid in my mind like yesterday, but it's been about twelve years. I went deep into the jungle with shamans, and took ayahuasca."

"What's ayahuasca?"

"A powerful plant medicine that opened up my mind like nothing else. During a ceremony, the whole idea of this garden came to me as a download of information. It generated a deeper understanding of nature's neural networks."

Cyndra's eyebrows lifted with a look of disbelief on her face.

"Trust me, it's very real."

"Is that when you started this garden?"

"There was no time to waste. I had the idea and as it turned out, I got the funding that made it possible." Daemon's voice trailed off. He became quiet and distant for a moment. He recalled his parents' death from an automobile accident, and their will naming him as full beneficiary.

Leaves and branches brushed against the crew and tractors as they moved through the paths. "We're now moving through the Energeia Garden, loaded with stimulant plants." He pointed out some of his favorites, like guarana vines. Their red fruit naturally opened up when ripe, revealing black seeds outlined in white, resembling watchful eyes. "We'll soon be near the center, where all the gardens meet. That's where I believe we can find the unfolding of Utopia."

Once at the core of the garden, the tractors stopped. A large pond sat ahead of them. Everyone shoveled the rock powder mix from the trailers onto the ground near the trees and other plants on either side of the path. Armando and his team started on an adjacent path. The tractors gradually moved forward as the workers completed each section. By the end of the first run, everyone was dripping with sweat.

"We need to get this finished by mid-day, there's two more projects that need to be completed after this," Daemon reminded them.

"Piece of cake," said Armando, attempting to boost morale.

Daemon and Cyndra shoveled rock powder in the same area. She maneuvered energetically through vines and other brush, creating a dust cloud around her. Overhead, a boisterous flock of Quaker parrots stole her attention with their lively chatter. She stood still as the active birds propelled themselves from one branch to another, chopping the air with their wings. Unexpectedly, she released a scream for help. Ants blanketed her legs from her shoes up to her thighs.

Daemon raced to Cyndra, as she slapped and brushed her legs. "Fire ants," he said, helping her away from the dome shaped nest. Small, reddish brown invaders poured out of their mound, as if the ground itself flowed like living lava. Daemon's hands swept away any remaining ants on her body.

"Ouch, those bites really hurt." Welts grew all over her legs, and her brow furrowed.

"Don't worry, you'll feel better soon," he said, grabbing a first aid kit from the tractor. Squeezing some red gel on his hands, he caressed her legs, which glistened from the cooling balm.

"Why is the gel so red?" Cyndra asked.

"It's dragon's blood extract. We grow the trees here; they have a natural blood red sap that's excellent for treating skin conditions like this."

"I don't understand how I got covered with ants so suddenly." Her mouth grimaced and her gaze was scattered.

"They're not that speedy; instead, they utilize stealth." Daemon looked down for a moment, making sure they were not being advanced upon by anymore of those tiny warriors.

"But I felt the stings all at once," she said, her hands trembling.

"That's part of their strategy for greater impact. They sneak onto their target, and on cue, they all sting simultaneously."

"That's gross." She took the container and dabbed on more dragon's blood herself. "Can't you get rid of them?"

"Even if I could in a safe organic way, I wouldn't want to," Daemon said adamantly.

"Why not?"

"Like it or not, they are incredibly efficient recyclers. Being an omnivore, they consume practically everything. Seeds, fruit, other insects, even baby vertebrates are on the menu. They assimilate a wide spectrum of life, and that's valuable for the garden."

"That sounds a little weird." Her gaze shifted down to the burning bumps on her legs.

"It's definitely not mainstream. It's about creating a natural environment in a way that maximizes transformation."

"I'm still not sure what you mean."

"Transformation is the essence of life. Good recyclers like ants, contribute to creating rich ecosystems, abundant with life energy. Plus, the chemistry of their stings acts like an accelerant to this process."

"Still sounds a little crazy, especially with the stinging." Her azure gaze grew more fixed.

"Actually, there is some medical benefit to the ant stings, they treat psoriasis and other auto-immune conditions."

"Alright, I give up," she exclaimed, throwing her hands in the air, "fire ants are okay."

It didn't take long for Daemon's natural treatment to work its magic, and Cyndra returned to enriching the garden. The team continued to exert themselves until they finished the job, then took a well-deserved lunch break.

Cyndra walked toward her house with one of the crew members, Emilio. She looked on as he scanned photos on his phone. "I don't think it's fair that Daemon lets you have your phone in the garden."

"I actually work for Armando, he's more reasonable," Emilio said as he sent out some plant photos. He then moved to photos of their activity today, and posted them on social media.

Cyndra saw herself in one of the group photos with everyone covered in dust. "Don't post that. We look like zombies."

Emilio held out his phone, wanting to get a close up. "Hold still."

"Put it down now, and nobody gets hurt." Her arm reached forward with her hand in a playfully defiant fist.

Emilio slid the phone back into his pocket.

"So, who's interested in plant photos?"

"A lady named Mara Blackstone. Believe it or not, she pays me to send these pics. You know, she could practically take them herself, since she lives next door."

"What? You mean someone living in El Dorado? Everybody there is rich. Dude, how'd you get so connected?"

"Just through a friend who works for them." He paused for a moment and smiled. "I've got big news. Are you ready? Mrs. Blackstone is having a party this Wednesday night, and *you're* invited!"

"Are you kidding? Why me?"

"She likes this jungle garden, and wants to show some appreciation to the people who work here. Her and her husband are really cool, and you for sure won't believe their house." He pulled out a dirty card from his pocket with Mara's information on it. "Send her a text, let her know you're coming."

"Okay... sure... thanks." Still not quite believing it. "Are you going?"

"I'd like to, but it's my girl-friend's birthday; she's got other plans. Enjoy your break," he said, heading to the shed for lunch with the rest of the crew.

Cyndra slid her thumb across the dusty card, revealing Mara's name along with a company name, Psi-Matics Global.

She stepped inside her house, and took a deep refreshing breath of cool air. Her skin tingled, but muscles panged throughout her body. It was only mid-day and she had already shoveled and spread many times her own weight in minerals. Completely covered in dust, she caught a glimpse of herself in a full length mirror, and gasped. She *did* look like a zombie. Her skin was gritty from the combination of dust and sweat. She immediately slid out of her clothes, and scooted to the shower. Afterwards, wrapped in a thick soft towel, she said hello to her fleecy roommate in the kitchen. Nisha meowed hungrily.

"Looks like you could use a special treat today," she said, opening a can of fancy cat food, and spooned it in her bowl. Cyndra threw on some clothes and ate while catching up on her phone. Her lunch hour vanished too quickly, and she returned to discover what other torturous activities Daemon had in store for them.

"Cut down all the angel's trumpet trees, grind them up in the wood chipper, and then spread it out as mulch," Daemon ordered.

Angel's trumpet trees occupied a significant portion of the Morpheus Garden, and they grew in other gardens as well. Blowers scattered most bees off of the flowers, or the crew simply picked off the flowers. Armando operated the chipper. The others were cutting their way through the angel's trumpet forest, leaving only stumps about knee height. Daemon assisted with the cutting and made sure everything was done correctly. Armando took a break from the chipper, and Daemon came over.

"Making progress," Daemon said as they both relaxed for a minute. "That's quite a pile of wood chips."

"Emilio *was* moving it. What's taking him so long?" Armando asked.

"Keep your eye on Emilio, there's something suspicious about him."

Mara stood behind her house facing Daemon's forested property. Her phone displayed the text message, *be there soon*. She then saw Emilio hoisting himself over the cinder block wall separating Elysium Jungle and El Dorado Village. "Emilio, come here," she called, waving her arm.

Standing together, Mara directed his attention upwards to the second story area of her house. "Have you ever seen anything like that?"

Emilio's jaw dropped as he spied the new development on the wall. "Wow, that's a monster," he gasped.

Directly on the outside surface of Mara's house, a massive swarm of honey bees built their nest, but in an odd arrangement. The fresh yellow honeycombs formed three concentric circles, and the entire thing spanned four feet across.

"What do you think is going on?" Mara asked.

"I don't know," he said, scratching his head. "It looks like a big target."

"A bee removal service is scheduled to arrive later today." Her eyes sparkled bright green as her gaze turned. "What's that tangled mess?" she asked, pointing toward a tree in her yard. "I've seen it growing in Daemon's garden, it must have come from there." The tree held what looked like long green spaghetti running through its branches.

"They call it love vine. It's a parasitic plant," he said.

"Why is Daemon growing parasitic plants?"

"I don't know, I just try not to get lost in there."

"Let's go inside, out of this heat, and see what you have for me."

Standing in the foyer, Emilio reached into his pocket and pulled out a sandwich size plastic bag packed full of ground up flowers, leaves and twigs. "Here you go, angel's trumpet, nice 'n fresh from the grinder." He handed her the small bag with big potential.

"Thank you for this, and also for giving Cyndra the invitation." Mara handed him some folded cash and stepped in closer. "Come back later today, after Elysium is closed. I have something for you to distribute throughout Daemon's garden. No one else needs to know."

"Yes, Mrs. Blackstone, I'll be here," he said as he left.

"Keep sending photos," she said, as he walked toward the wall, returning to the grind.

Mara picked up her phone and called Jack Landon. "I'm having honeycombs removed from my house; just another item to add to our list of concerns with Elysium."

"Be careful, I just got another report of someone getting stung multiple times," he said.

"More importantly, I'm sending several hundred

photos from Daemon's actual garden, not just the tour garden, to our professor friend at Caloosa University to take a look at them. I want to know if anything is growing there that shouldn't be, legally speaking. We'll eventually find something."

As Mara finished the call, Griff stepped into the room. "Shall we program the shipment?" he asked, his arms wrapped around a box that had just arrived from Guatemala.

"Let's go," she said, and they trudged upstairs.

They entered a room, where against one wall was a large electronic apparatus. A computer displayed an array of functions including power output, frequency, audio, and more. Griff approached the large telescoping lens structure with concentric rings that faced the wall toward Daemon's property. "You said the bees are really attracted to the magnetic field outside the house?"

"Yes, but the bee removal service said their treatment should keep them away, at least for a few months," said Mara.

"Good, we should be done by then." Griff set the box down onto a sensitized plate, and turned on the device. "I understand the process could be more thorough if their bodies were in direct contact with the plate, but I think if we just leave it on longer it will work okay through the box."

Mara nodded. Just the thought of taking out the contents and handling them seemed repellant.

Griff adjusted the settings, and let them get immersed in the holographic, quantum entanglement technology. "This is an opportune time to program life forms, when they're already in a state of metamorphosis."

"Daemon's garden will never be the same," she said, smiling. "He's searching for illumination, but he's only going to find more darkness."

Afternoon clouds took the edge off of the oppressive summer sun. The angel trumpet forest was nothing but stumps, and the resulting mulch blanketed areas near the garden's center. Daemon enlisted Armando to start the final job of the day; spraying microbes.

"Yesterday, I started several buckets of microbes in the lab. They should be ready to spray onto the angel's trumpet mulch," said Daemon.

"Got it," said Armando who enlisted Emilio to help. It was good timing to spread the microbes late in the day, avoiding harsh sunlight that could kill them. Bacteria broke down the minerals and other nutrients, accelerating their availability to the plants. The team finally finished and plodded to the parking area, ready to go home and crash.

Daemon and Cyndra walked together. "Would you like to join me for dinner tonight?" he asked.

"Nope," replied Cyndra, looking straight ahead. "Staying home and recovering."

"Okay then," he said with some disappointment. "See you tomorrow morning for the photo shoot."

Feeling refreshed later in the evening, Cyndra decided to go for a short run. She felt like it would loosen her up after all that drudgery. Wearing her running shoes, she sprinted around the tour garden.

Although it was dark, the yard lights along the sidewalk illuminated her path. She felt good and picked up speed.

Her feet pounded against the concrete surface. Overhanging branches came and went. She moved into a more effortless flow. Forgetting about everything else while running, her mind relaxed. Ahead on the curving pathway, dark shapes moved in various directions. As she closed in, it became apparent they were cane toads. She watched her step, however, one toad jumped out in front of her as her foot came down, and she squashed it. Cyndra slipped on the disemboweled creature, and fell on the concrete with a thud and a shriek. Her backside throbbed, and her hands stung.

This took her back to a summer of trepidation in Indiana, when she was seven years old. Her mother was away with temporary employment, leaving her alone with her father. It was a hot, humid evening. She quietly stepped outside, with tears in her eyes. Standing and trembling on their large back porch she spotted a beautiful green tree frog sitting on the hand railing. Her father followed, "My little free spirit, you need to keep our secret, or bad things can happen." He clenched his hand into a fist, and smashed it down onto the frog. With a pop and squish, white and red liquids shot out from under the edges of his hand. She gasped, then held her breath. "Get in the house, princess," he said, grabbing her by the arm. Once inside, he locked the door behind them.

Cyndra helped herself up to standing. Taking a deep breath, she spoke quietly to herself, "It's over…I'm here now." She scraped off the slimy residue from the sole of her shoe, then hobbled back to her house; *it's going to be okay.*

Day Four

"Wisdom begins in wonder."
Socrates

The soft light of a new day fell on Daemon and Cyndra standing in the tour garden. At their side stood a man holding a camera, and a woman with a microphone.

"Daemon, you're growing a wide range of mind enhancing plants, nootropics as you call them," said the interviewer. "What makes Elysium Jungle's nootropics so special?"

"A big factor is the parasitic plants," Daemon said. He pointed out a guava tree with its white flowers, then to an area of the tree where magenta and green flowers appeared on branches with differently shaped leaves. "That's a tropical mistletoe growing out of the guava."

Parasitic plants derived water and nutrients from other plants. Daemon pulled back the bushy branches adorned with colorful blooms and revealed a thick root system covering the tree trunk. Small structures on the parasitic roots penetrated the host plant and absorbed not only water and minerals, but also phytonutrients, alkaloids, and various medicinal chemicals from their hosts. Many parasitic plants produced their own sugars through photosynthesis, thus known as semi-parasitic plants.

Daemon moved to an area of higher ground, and stood next to a soft green bush adorned with lilac flowers. "Here is a rock rose that has a parasitic plant growing in its roots; and there's its flower." He pointed toward the ground where a corn cob shaped form emerged from the earth, covered in hundreds of tiny wine colored flowers. "Although it's called Maltese mushroom, it is not a fungus but a fully parasitic plant, which has no chlorophyll." Fully parasitic plants did not utilize photosynthesis, and depended on their host plant for everything. Daemon typically did not make an outward distinction between semi and fully parasitic, simply calling all of them parasitic.

Medicinal plants being parasitized often produced a larger quantity of their therapeutic chemicals due to the stress response. Also, when a parasitic plant absorbed and combined curative elements from other plants, its own chemical profile changed.

"Please continue about the relevance of parasitic plants to your work," she said.

"They create new combinations of nootropics that have their own unique effects, and they actually assimilate new, never before seen, mind enhancing compounds. We're taking nootropics to a new level."

"Could you further explain?"

Daemon stepped over to a desert sandalwood tree, bearing round, scarlet fruit. Around the tree grew two species of small bushy plants, one with purple flowers and the other white. "This sandalwood is hosting on these astragalus and licorice plants, taking in their medicinal values. Its fruit and nuts are now receiving longevity factors from the astragalus and energizing qualities from the licorice." Through the connections

59

with parasitic plants, even the host plants shared in the exchange of chemistry from the other plants, expanding the potential for all. "Practically the entire garden is synthesizing new medicinals," Daemon explained.

"Off camera, you mentioned the microbiome of the soil. Could you say something about that?"

"I have developed new strains of soil bacteria and rapidly growing Mycorrhizal fungi, that also exchange chemical information." Daemon reached down and pulled up a chunk of mulch, revealing the white thread-like mycelium of the fungi growing beneath the soil's surface. He described how mycorrhizal fungi symbiotically connected to plants through their roots, exchanging nutrients. Over time, the mycorrhizal fungi spread and merged with other mycorrhizal fungi, ultimately creating a vast pathway for nutrient flow, networking everything together, like an ecosystem internet.

"Although you can't see them, there are plenty of bacteria, almost one billion per spoonful of soil." Important recyclers of nutrients, bacteria also performed other functions. Purple non-Sulphur bacteria produced monoatomic elements, supporting the nervous system. Magnetic bacteria increased plant growth and vitality.

"Looks like you're farming below ground as well as above ground," stated the interviewer.

"Get the soil right, and the plants take care of themselves. We have all kingdoms of life in harmony."

The interviewer turned to Cyndra. "What do you like about working here?"

"I enjoy working in a natural, beautiful environment.

It also keeps me in great physical condition. Yesterday, I helped shovel tons of sand and chop up a small forest of trees. Maintaining paradise is meaningful work, but it's also really hard work."

Daemon moved in to the camera. "Cyndra is a wonderful new addition to our staff, and there is a bit of a learning curve. Yesterday, we did have an unusually heavy work load. But, compared to other farms, Elysium Jungle is actually low maintenance."

"Low maintenance?" exclaimed Cyndra, frowning. "Compared to what?" She folded her arms. "Other places must be murderous."

The interviewer spoke up, "Okay, I think we have enough, that's a wrap. We'll send some demos for your approval." They quickly packed up and left.

Lynette, observing from the sidelines, stepped forward. "You came off being so professional and thought provoking," she said. "I already have a list of companies to send the video to."

Daemon gave his young assistant a quick hug. "I think Cyndra looked great in the video. Lynette, you've got an amazing niece, so capable and willing to do anything."

Cyndra glanced at Daemon. "Thanks, you help me go beyond what I think I'm capable of doing."

Lynette spoke up, "I have an announcement. I'm going to Indiana to visit my sister Molly; Cyndra's mom." She took a deep breath and centered herself. "Cyndra, did you get a message from her?"

"I saw that mom called," Cyndra said, becoming still and quiet.

"Molly's been through a tough time, but it sounds like she's turning it around. I wanted to be there and support her. Cyndra, you know deep inside she really loves you."

"Yeah, sure," she said, looking down, her voice barely audible.

"I'll be leaving tonight, and will be gone about a week. Don't worry Daemon, I'll still be looking into the funding while I'm gone." She gave them both a hug and left.

As she walked away, Armando walked toward them. "What's up for today?" he asked.

"Please take Cyndra to the greenhouse and show her that part of the operation," Daemon instructed. "I'll meet up with you soon."

The atmosphere of the greenhouse carried the fresh, sweet scent of new life. During the first few years of creating the garden, Daemon used the greenhouse to start many trees and bushes. He planted seeds and seedlings, and grew them to a large enough size to be transplanted outside. That stage in the development of the garden was fairly complete. Currently, he focused more on starting vines and epiphytes to grow on the established trees, filling any available niche with more diversity and productivity.

"I forgot to say, you both did an excellent job enriching the garden yesterday," said Daemon.

"You got your money's worth," Armando said, rubbing his shoulder.

"I didn't realize there were so many *Brugmansia*

trees in your garden," Cyndra said. "I think you've got more angel's trumpets than heaven itself."

"Thank you both for doing the heavy lifting," said Daemon, as his gaze focused upon Cyndra. "How do you like the greenhouse?"

"It's so calm and quiet in here. Like a little Shangri-La. No bugs or blistering sun, just beautiful plants with youthful energy." Her turquoise eyes shimmered.

Daemon turned toward Armando. "How's the *Gaiadendron punctatum* doing?"

Daemon's favorite parasitic epiphyte, *Gaiadendron punctatum*, fed on other epiphytes such as orchids and bromeliads. Growing on trees, epiphytes generally did not have roots that extended into the ground, making it difficult for other parasitic plants to access their chemistry. Gaiadendron provided the solution to getting epiphytes connected, as it fed specifically on them. In addition, its roots extended downward into the ground, taking the mind enhancing nootropics derived from the air plants, and sharing them with the other parasitic plants throughout the garden.

"Your vampire plants are doing good on bark medium," said Armando. "Some ready for transplant into the trees."

"Excellent. You've gotten many seedlings from the parent plant in the garden. How is that plant doing?" Daemon asked.

"Very good, many blooms."

"Could you harvest some of the Vanda tessellata orchid that it's connected with. I look forward to its tranquilizing effects."

63

"Okay, tomorrow morning."

"Have the African dream herb vines germinated?"

"Yes. Cyndra, show Daemon the plants you watered," he said, pointing to the other side of the room.

Daemon and Cyndra walked quietly on the soft, sandy ground of the greenhouse to the area with the dream herbs. They observed a dozen slender green shoots reaching for the sky. "They look so tender and vulnerable, but each will grow into a massive vine, with a base as thick as your thigh," said Daemon. "They're powerful dream herbs." He described how dream herbs enhanced dreams, without otherwise affecting the mind, except sometimes inducing drowsiness. They also increased the possibility for lucid dreaming, where the dreamer becomes awake in their dream. He looked deeply into Cyndra's eyes. "Would you like to experiment with dream inducing herbs?"

"I guess, but I usually don't have any dreams," she answered.

"You'll be surprised at how extraordinary your dreams can be."

"Sounds interesting."

"I have a guest arriving shortly, and he'll be leaving about eight. Be at my place by nine, with an open mind and an empty stomach."

Over the years, preoccupied with his garden, Daemon had failed to keep in touch with Azarias, a friend of his parents, who sometimes watched over Daemon as a child. Azarias would visit them at their home in Tampa, from his place in nearby Tarpon Springs. Through

Daemon's childhood and teen years, he had admired Azarias' positive outlook and insight. Daemon needed the support of a wise elder more than ever, and so he reconnected with Azarias, and requested his astute counsel. They caught up on each other's lives walking together in the garden. Azarias moved with a quiet power; not so much of the body, but of the mind and spirit. Yet, it was palpable, like a physical energy. His grey hair was sleeked back. His face etched with lines of wisdom, with eyes alert and focused.

"This southerly location is even more tropical than Tarpon Springs. I've never seen so much variety of plants and wildlife," Azarias said as they explored Elysium.

"Thanks for noticing, it's something I strive for. One way that's accomplished is by optimizing the Permaculture concept of 'edge'," Daemon replied.

Edge described the space where two different habitats merged, such as the shoreline between land and water. That boundary area supported more life than either the aquatic or terrestrial alone. Inhabitants there included aquatic animals like frogs and turtles, overlapping with terrestrial animals like racoons and song birds. It supported a great diversity of plants as well."

Fluorescent red and yellow flowers of tropical mistletoes made Azarias pause. "The fusion of species with the parasitic plants is especially fascinating. You're like a biological alchemist."

"Thanks, but perhaps I've placed too much emphasis on transforming the environment, and not enough on myself."

"If you're capable of doing this much with the natural world, you certainly have the capacity to re-create your own inner world."

"Whatever advice or teachings you have to offer me would be deeply appreciated."

"I can advise, but you must do the work," he said, brushing away small branches that crossed the pathway.

They circled back to Daemon's house to cool off. Azarias relaxed on the couch while Daemon prepared pineapple sage tea.

"I'm giving you several meditations to practice every day." He took a sip of the hot tea. "Ahh, very fruity."

"It's calming and neuro-regenerative," said Daemon, compelled to share information about his plants, as usual.

"Spend at least 20 minutes with each meditation, maybe more. Have your sessions at the beginning of the day, and again at night." His tone was serious.

Daemon leaned in, listening intently.

"First thing in the morning, mantra meditation," he said with authority. "Choose a word or phrase that has meaning for you, say for instance, Utopia Nectar, and repeat it over and over. You can do part of it out loud, part of it internally, and not only saying the words, but also listening to them."

"That sounds almost too easy," Daemon said, stretching out his arms.

"Do the practice and see, it might surprise you," said Azarias with a slight smile. "Also listen for your mind's response, especially phrases or words that are in conflict with it, like 'that's too difficult', 'it doesn't feel right,' or 'it's unknowable.'

"Do you think focusing on those negative ideas will be helpful?" Daemon asked.

"Extremely helpful. Contradictory words or ideas that come up are your obstacles to discovery."

Daemon felt unnerved as if Azarias looked directly into his mind. He nodded, and had more tea.

Azarias cleared his throat as he began again. "The second meditation involves visualization. Are you capable of creating a mental picture?"

"Absolutely," Daemon replied. "I imagine things all the time."

"Good. Envision a powerful beam of light, filled with all the energy and information you need, coming down to you from the heavens. It shines down through the top of your head and into your heart. Feel it expand your heart. Generate the feelings that Utopia Nectar will bring to the world. Feel the happiness, contentment, and any other positive emotions associated with it. Feel grateful for it."

"Feelings are important in meditation?"

"Very much so. Emotions are magnetic, drawing your goals to you," he said as his hands moved slowly toward his heart. "You can imagine the light as gentle, or much more intense if you prefer, like a bolt of lightning, very powerful and immediate." Azarias sat back for a moment, and gazed out the window. A small tree stood close to Daemon's house. Bulbous, magenta flowers hung along the branches in rows. Some branches held round, yellow fruit. "What a beautiful tree, it seems to have a powerful presence."

"That's the Tree of Wizards, *Latua pubiflora*. It's a rare member of the nightshade family, used by shamans in Chile."

Azarias nodded, then finished his tea before explaining the last meditation. "Realize the power of breath to change your consciousness. Do some deep breathing. Feel abundance with the inhale, and squeeze your abdominals tight with the exhale. Become more aware of your abdomen, especially the solar plexus. Feel the strength and support from your core. Imagine it not only as physical strength but also energetic strength; will power and intention." He held his hands near his abdomen as if embracing energy.

Refreshed by the tea, they stepped out onto the lanai. Here, they enjoyed a vivid, close up view of nearby plants and trees, while protected from annoying bugs. Wild coffee, a glossy leaved native bush bore pure white, fragrant flowers that attracted zebra longwing butterflies. Their jet black wings, inscribed with radiant yellow stripes, flapped lazily as they floated around the aromatic bush.

Facing the garden, Azarias seemed to absorb its life energy directly. "This is a beautiful place; but remember its beauty is a reflection of your creativity and insight. It is your essence that ultimately is of value and worth cultivating, not so much the external result."

Daemon's face glowed, embracing a sense of empowerment from his mentor's inspiring words.

"The sun is setting; it's cooling off a bit. How about another walk?" asked Azarias.

The sun hid behind the trees, casting long deep shadows. A magical time unfolded when day merged with night, like a diversity rich permaculture edge. Here, however, the edge was not from mixing different habitats, but rather by blending the cycles of light and dark; a combination of diurnal and nocturnal activity. Immersed in the subdued glow of both worlds, they continued their exchange.

"How long has it been since you began Elysium Jungle?" asked Azarias.

"Eleven years. This month is actually the anniversary."

"That's quite a commitment. Also, the number eleven is about balancing superlative feminine and masculine energies."

"Sounds like my new student. She's definitely got super feminine energy. Could she be part of this equation?"

"She's with you at an auspicious time, and could be valuable in your journey. Learn from her, and keep opening up. At this point it's absolutely essential."

Daemon moved quietly, deeply considering the advice. "I want things to change, and actually they are."

"Tell me more." Their pace slowed.

"The nectars are becoming more potent. We are still using the same ingredients and proportions, but people are having more powerful results."

"Interesting," said Azarias. Movement overhead caught his attention. Looking up, he noticed white egrets gliding straight to their roost for the night, amid the erratic journey of awakened bats.

Daemon continued, "Another thing is that electronics tend to get unpredictable, especially around a full moon. We had to sub out our online sales. It's still profitable, but could be better."

"Sounds like interdimensional or portal energy." He paused, suspended in the uplifting fragrance from the stellar white flowers of a Milky Way Tree, *Stemmadenia littoralis*. "Your garden is otherworldly in so many ways."

"I feel this tingling in my feet, even into my legs. What do you think?" Daemon asked, stepping mindfully along the path.

"It's definitely a surge of earth energy. I feel it too."

They meandered through the darkening external world, and simultaneously, through an increasingly illuminated inner world. Daemon enjoyed an increased sense of confidence and direction in his quest. The moon, almost half in its journey of phases, rose into view.

"The new moon last week coincided with the cool front. I sensed a distinct shift of energy," said Azarias.

Daemon looked hopeful. "Good, I could use something new."

"This year, the full moon is going to be on the summer solstice. The moon and sun at their strongest the same day."

"Hmm. That's also the day Gaia is going into new ownership. My deadline."

"Powerful sun, full moon, and Utopia. After all that, you may never be the same."

Daemon and Cyndra sipped some dream enhancing blue lotus tea at his kitchen table. She appeared comfortable and radiant, wearing a simple white dress. Daemon wore a deep violet shirt, conscious of the color association with mind and dreams.

"This blue lotus tea tastes odd," said Cyndra. "Needs more honey." She poured a liberal amount into her cup. "Do you really think herbs will help me remember dreams?"

"These herbs will take you into dream heaven." He opened up a bottle of Morpheus Nectar. "Put two dropper fulls under your tongue, and let it sit there a moment before swallowing."

With dropper in hand, Cyndra tilted her head back, parting her lips, and extending her tongue. She squeezed out the liquid into her mouth and grimaced. Daemon prided himself on making the nectars tasty, however, the dream nectar turned out to be the least palatable of the group. She immediately washed it down with some water.

"Too bitter!" she said, and swished more water in her mouth.

"I admit, this one is an acquired taste." He leaned forward. "What would you like to dream?" His dark eyes more magnetic.

"I'd like dreams full of wonderful sensations, beautiful colors and textures, and inviting exotic places."

"Sounds delightful." He kept his gaze locked on hers as he took another sip of tea. Her slender form so vivacious, she appeared to practically hover over her chair. "The more aware we are of our dreams, the more aware we are of the subconscious mind."

"I want my dreams to be so vividly beautiful that I'll never forget them." She sipped more tea.

Despite Cyndra's alluring quality, Daemon couldn't help going into teacher mode. "Good, but I recommend that you drop the 'want' and instead, make it an intention. No wanting, which implies you need something. Rather, make a statement like you already have it. A positive statement, no negatives."

Cyndra paused for a moment considering her words. "You mean like, my dreams are so vividly beautiful I will always remember them," she said, sitting up tall.

"Perfect!" With the success of that small lesson, he gave himself permission to relax more fully.

"What about your dreams?" she asked, raising her eyebrows.

"Right now, I'm so focused on creating Utopia Nectar, I would like a dream that offers insight into that project."

"I'm sure you will create it. You're so determined, it just has to happen."

"Thanks, Cyndra, I appreciate your support. I don't have many people to share this with."

"Daemon, why *don't* you have more people in your life? You isolate yourself too much, hidden away in this jungle. You're a talented, attractive guy. Don't you want to get out more?"

"A part of me does, but as the years go by, I find myself sinking deeper into research." Daemon paused and closed his eyes for a moment. "I've been discovering more relationships between the living things in my garden, than with people." He took a deep breath. Daemon had expressed something to Cyndra that he rarely even admitted to himself. He felt a bit vulnerable. His hands squeezed together.

Cyndra looked into Daemon's despondent eyes. "It's okay." She reached out and placed her hand on his. They sat quietly for a few moments. Cyndra's shoulders softened, and she said quietly, "There's so much I don't know about you. What was your childhood like?"

Daemon's first response wanted to be *What does that have to do with anything?* but he knew it had everything to do with it. Should he try to maneuver away from the topic? Could he trust Cyndra? He decided to give her the positive spin.

"My parents were very giving. I received some nice things."

"They were generous, that sounds very loving," she said, assuring him.

There was another long quiet pause.

"Where are they now?"

Daemon spoke reluctantly, "They passed suddenly about twelve years ago. A car accident."

"I'm so sorry."

"It's okay, that was a long time ago." His voice trailed off. "Life goes on. And your childhood?" he asked, maneuvering to get out from being questioned.

"My dad disappeared when I was a young child. My mom supported me the best she could, I guess. Had some good times. But when I was sixteen, she fell and hurt her back and got hooked on opioids. It got pretty bad. I moved out the following year, and stayed with aunt Lynette. Haven't talked to mom much since then."

"Sorry to hear that." Daemon held Cyndra's hand. "What we do to improve our consciousness will help us heal."

Cyndra began to yawn, then caught herself. "Oh, I didn't mean to do that, you're not boring me."

"That's okay, it's the dream herbs, they're making you drowsy. Let's call it a night."

Daemon walked Cyndra back to her house. Insects and toads chattered through the soupy night air.

"Look at the moon," she said, pointing. "It's so moody with the dark clouds around it."

"It's spellbinding," said Daemon, trying to stay present, but with the residual tension from his quest growing tighter. The moon became like an indicator light, gradually getting brighter, and when full, Utopia would either be completed or abandoned.

Cyndra opened her door. "Good night, Daemon. Sweet, insightful dreams." Cyndra's gaze was full of longing, but also revealed a need for sleep. She drew her hand toward her mouth and yawned more fully.

"It has been a pleasure," he said with a warm smile. "May your dreams be thrilling." He waved and returned home. The scent of night blooming jasmine enhanced his thoughts of her, sending chills up his spine.

Inside, he stayed up a bit longer, researching the illuminati, who were connected with the Free Masons. He read almost unbelievable accounts of illuminati parents traumatizing their children, short circuiting their ability to feel empathy and compassion. They conditioned their next generation to be like themselves, basically parasitic psychopaths, feeding off humanity. Daemon reflected on the seemingly endless cycles of abuse among this powerful group toward each other, and the rest of the world. *How long before humanity wakes up to who these people really are?*

Turning off the computer, Daemon disengaged from his esoteric cyber world. Turning his attention toward a review of his day, he cherishing his time with Azarias, and also unwound from the difficult sharing with Cyndra of his childhood. His tired eyes and sluggish body signaled time to sleep, and he quickly found himself entering that ethereal world.

Daemon laid face up in his crib, unable to move, surrounded by circles of candles and shadowy figures. A gel-like substance with a chemical smell covered his forehead. The sticky material seemed to catch the voices around him, and channeled the sound through his forehead and deeply into his brain. The flaming circles expanded into vast pathways bleached under a tropical sun. The voices morphed into the calls of birds and insects inhabiting a lush forest. The synthetic scent blossomed into more natural aromatic tones. A large deep well marked the center of the concentric walkways. Looming over it, he peered down into the dark, bottomless space. He shuddered as it generated a compulsive spinning, like an underworld tornado siphoning off his soul.

Daemon's body shook as he awoke, as if trying to

catch himself from falling. Relieved it was just a dream, but puzzled about its true nature. Rather than something he imagined, it felt more like an event he remembered.

Day Five

"The hidden harmony is more powerful than the obvious."
Heraclitus

In the late morning, Katashi pulled up in a van loaded with research equipment. He believed strongly in Daemon's work, and planned to stay and assist with using the complex apparatus. Daemon and Shavonda stepped out of the lab to greet him.

"It's so good to finally meet you," said Shavonda, clasping hands. "Daemon raves about your work at the main lab."

"It's just one logical step at a time," Katashi said, "right, Daemon?"

"Logic is good," said Daemon, as he opened the doors to the van, "but don't forget intuition."

Unloading the vehicle, small careful steps were taken with the boxes filled with delicate instruments. They placed everything on the large counter in the middle of the lab, and set it up without delay.

Among the equipment, a large, stainless steel mass spectrometer occupied a position of importance. Its ability to identify chemicals in extracts would be invaluable. In addition, the spectrometer interfaced with a high end, desktop computer utilizing strong artificial intelligence. This enhanced software searched the internet, providing the most up to date analysis of the chemical's effects on consciousness. The monitor displayed a diagram of the brain, highlighting particular areas known to be affected by any drug. In addition, written information scrolled down in a column along the right side

Shavonda gazed at this new, upgraded look to Daemon's lab, and glanced at Katashi. "Wow, this looks a little intimidating."

"Don't worry, it's surprisingly user friendly."

"Yeah, if the user is you," she replied.

Katashi brushed his straight black bangs away from his brow as he looked down at his screen, securing his internet connection. "Got it." He looked up at Daemon. "Do you have a back-up in case the power goes out?"

"Funny you should ask; I've got an emergency generator arriving soon." He took a step back, taking it all in. "I'll be prepared for anything."

Double checking all systems and information on multiple screens, Katashi looked ready. "Time for a test run."

Shavonda picked up a small bottle of extract. "This is one of my favorites." She inserted the prepared liquid into the spectrometer.

On the screen, the grey colored, modeled image of the brain began to light up in the prefrontal cortex and the parietal cortex. "It's working," said Katashi. Text appeared; elucidating all of its chemical constituents, theobromine, caffeine, serotonin, and phenethylamine among others. It indicated mental focus and alertness, combined with a euphoric element.

Daemon observed the screen indicating its final

analysis. "That's what I thought, cacao."

"You can also move the image," said Katashi, grabbing the mouse. "It's 3D. View it from different angles."

Daemon's face lit up, observing the front of the brain to the back, as well as one hemisphere to the other. "That's quite impressive."

"Not only that," clicking away with the mouse, "you can even look deeper inside the brain. You can see what's happening with the pineal gland, the corpus callosum, the cerebrum and more. It's practically unlimited."

"This is a game changer," said Daemon, rubbing his hands together. "Considering the recent increase in plant potency, we need new harvests, to make powerful, up to date extracts for testing."

A knock at the door revealed a burly man who asked, "Is this the site for the emergency generator?"

Daemon directed him with the details of the installation.

"Mister, for just a little more, you could've gotten a bigger generator, it would easily handle everything here."

"All I need covered is the equipment on the table," Daemon replied.

"Alright. Whatever."

Daemon returned to the main room, and pulled Cyndra aside. "Come with me, it's time you found out more about the nectars," he said, and led her into the production room.

They walked over to a small but automated

production line system. At the beginning of the line there were empty nectar bottles along with jars filled with various types of extracts and honey. There was a packaging station at the other end with boxes, tape, a scale, and other materials for shipping. Daemon gathered up four dispensers filled with honey, and placed them on a table. They each contained honey collected from his four gardens. One was derived from stimulant plants, another from sedative plants and so forth. Each was used to make the corresponding nectar. For instance, honey collected from the stimulant garden, was combined with extracts from stimulating plants, in order to make Energeia Nectar.

"Honey is liquid gold," Daemon said, explaining the benefits of honey, an important ingredient in the nectars. Honey contained vitamins, minerals, anti-oxidants and flavonoids. The sugars and enzymes functioned as an excellent delivery system, carrying nutrients into cells. Honey energized the body, plus it helped stabilize glucose levels. He invited her to take some honey from the Energeia garden, and really taste it. Cyndra opened her mouth and tilted her head back. Her tongue reached out, covering her bottom lip, and a slender golden stream poured onto it.

"How is it?" Daemon asked.

"Delicious," Cyndra replied, licking her lips. "With a slight spiciness."

"It looks like you're enjoying this lecture," he said.

"I like sweet talk," she said and smiled.

They continued to converse and taste their way through the rest of the honeys, feeding mind and body.

"Obviously, honey is amazing, but not all honey is safe. Depending on the type of flowers it's harvested from, it can have serious consequences." He guided her to a secured wooden cabinet. Reaching into a nearby drawer, he pulled out a key, and unlocked it. Inside revealed jars of honey of varying hues from deep gold to umber.

He pulled a jar off the shelf. "This is from *Rhododendron ponticum,* along with a Florida native, *R. viscosum*, the swamp azalea. Their flowers are spicy like cloves." Daemon became dreamy eyed for a moment. "A flavorful honey, however, it contains grayanotoxins."

Grayanotoxins caused overstimulation of the central nervous system, a type of inebriation. Some people reported psychedelic effects. For others, it increased sexual performance or helped with arthritis. There could be other results like blurred vision, weakness, and change in heart rhythm. It's popular in Nepal, where plenty of rhododendron are found. There, the giant Himalayan Honeybee produced and stored it in huge honeycombs that hung on mountain cliffs. Psychedelic effects or not, just collecting it was a trip. It went by the name mad honey.

"So, this is my home grown version of madness." He unscrewed the lid and invited Cyndra to take in the fragrance of this beautiful but unpredictable golden liquid.

Cyndra tilted her head forward. "It's like perfume."

"That's right," he said, then returned it and pulled out another jar.

"What do we have this time?"

81

"A honey enjoyed by the Mayans. It's source is a woody vine in the morning glory family; the species is Rivea corymbosa."

The Aztecs called it snake plant. It had small, white, fragrant flowers, and was native to Mexico and tropical America. Not unusual for the morning glory family, it produced a hypnotic state, possibly visions. The active ingredient was ergot alkaloids, the original source for LSD.

"Although I've never taken a psychedelic, I have a friend who took LSD. What do you think about it?" Cyndra asked.

"I prefer natural plant medicines over synthetics, which have unknown long term effects. Plants, however, have been taken and studied for hundreds if not thousands of years."

"Daemon, have you ever used LSD?"

"Back in the day, I did try it a few times. I haven't done anything strong like that in many years. More and more I appreciate the gentle effectiveness of nootropics. Over the long term, it can be a deeper and more workable life transformation than using the extreme mind altering plants."

"I see what you're saying about nootropics being valuable. But why do you have so many psychedelics in your garden? It took six of us half a day to cut back your angel's trumpet forest, including the mulching and spreading. And you've got other types of psychedelics out there too. I know it's not just for looks. C'mon Daemon, what's up with all the mind bending plants?"

"There are two parts to that answer. One is that the

parasitic plants deliver trace amounts of psychedelics into the nootropic plants. It's like micro dosing, just enough to boost the effects of the nootropics, nothing beyond that." Daemon's voice became more quiet. "The other reason is a little esoteric, but you asked. Psychedelics are the most conscious members of the plant world, and consciousness has an effect on everything around it. Their presence alone upgrades the quality of the nectars; they bring a higher vibe to the whole garden."

Cyndra's mouth was hanging open a bit as she took in that unexpected information. "What happened when we got rid of all the angel's trumpets?"

"After getting pressured from El Dorado to get rid of their flowers, I realized how beneficial it would be to mulch them into the garden and spread that energy to other plants. It was a win win. Besides, they'll grow back quickly."

Cyndra paused, her eyelids half closed. After a few moments, she looked toward the cabinet. "Anymore strange honeys?"

"Yes, I've saved the worst for last, Yellow Jasmine, *Gelsemium sempervirens*. It's a psychedelic, but it also causes complete paralysis of all voluntary muscles.

Daemon explained how some tribal people had used this plant as a means of torture. They paralyzed their prisoners with it, then buried them alive up to their head. Ants would crawl on them, and into their nasal passages and throat, to the point where the prisoners choked to death. The victims were alive, awake, and able to feel everything, but unable to move a muscle.

Daemon added, "What a terrible way to go. I can barely imagine how vulnerable you would feel."

"Ugh, that sounds so ridiculously horrible. How can people be so brutal?"

"It's about psychopaths and domination over others. The world is a blend of dark and light. Nature allows that kind of energy to exist. This plant is a brutal teacher. You are forced to go beyond what you think is possible, or perhaps die."

"Do you ever take any of these?"

"I've taken extremely small amounts of each one, and so noticed only subtle effects from them. Mostly I keep them as a curiosity. Maybe one day I will learn how to use them in a healing way."

"I'm sure you will, maybe sooner than you think."

"Thanks for the positive sentiment... I think." He brushed his bangs back. "Switching gears, would you be interested in exploring the sensory enhancing qualities of Eros Nectar?

She tilted her head. "Hmmm, what exactly do you mean?"

"There is a certain intelligence and neural programming associated with pleasurable sensations. This is an opportunity to rewire cravings, and utilize passion to support the realization of positive goals."

"I'm open to try it." Her eyes sparkled.

"Good. Let's do a little harvesting tomorrow morning, and investigate the possibilities more deeply tomorrow night."

Cyndra indulged herself with a shower, its lukewarm

water refreshed her body and mind. Ever since childhood, she's had a strong urge to be as clean and fresh as possible. Afterwards, wearing a bath robe, she attended to Nisha, meowing with plenty of spirit.

Afterwards, she grabbed the cat wand toy with a feather attached at the end. She twirled it around Nisha, as the cat's gaze darted, following its movement. "Nisha looks so soft and cute." The feline suddenly pounced on the feather with sharp claws extended. "But look out, she's a fierce hunter."

Noticing the time, Cyndra readied herself for the party. She got on her phone and scheduled a ride. Getting dressed, she wondered who was this couple, Mara and Griff? Did they really want to meet her? Maybe she underestimated the value of Daemon's place. Working here was perhaps more prestigious than she thought.

As she entered El Dorado Village, the final rays of sunset tinted the opulent homes with golden light. The Blackstone's house was immense, looking twice as tall as a two story home should, and cast a long, deep shadow. Lights on the ground switched on, dramatically illuminating palms and other trees from their base up. The landscaping was flawless, not a leaf out of place.

"Welcome, Cyndra. We're so glad you could make it," said Mara, wearing a black dress, accented with an ornate gold necklace, and matching earrings. "Would you like something to drink?" she asked, as she gestured toward the ballroom. "The bartender is serving a wide range of drinks, including plenty of fresh fruit juices. I'll catch up to you in a few minutes."

Cyndra was impressed with the spaciousness of the rooms. She immersed herself in the luxurious quality of everything there. Polished marble floors, hand crafted antique furniture, and an eclectic blend of both contemporary and traditional sculpture and painting. It was more like an upscale museum than a home. A live quartet performed a romantic composition in the music room, filling the house with rich tonal qualities. At the bar, her lips pressed firmly onto a straw as she indulged in a virgin strawberry daiquiri. While sipping her sugary drink, a man approached her.

"Hi, you must be Cyndra, I'm Griff," he said as he leaned in for a light kiss on the cheek.

"Ah, nice to meet you," she said, "and thanks for the invitation. You have such an amazing home." She siphoned off more of her sweet, icy, beverage.

"It keeps us out of the rain." A trace of a smile crossed his thin lips. "Do you mind if I take your picture?" He pulled a phone out of his pocket.

"Oh, sure, go ahead."

Griff tapped, swiped, and maneuvered on his screen. "Hang on a minute, just getting the settings right." With a look of frustration, he finally spoke into the phone, "Record electromagnetic signature." He held the phone up and it emitted a beep.

"What did you mean, 'record electromagnetic signature'?" she asked.

He slid the phone back into his pocket. "Ah... what I meant was, I wanted to capture your attractive, magnetic quality." His head lightly bobbed in a reassuring gesture.

She glanced around the room, then asked, "Is anyone else here from Elysium Jungle?"

"Well, we know Emilio, and he told us how capable you are. Frankly, we're only looking for the best..." His gaze turned. "Please excuse me, I have something to give to a friend."

Cyndra wandered about, but mingling was somewhat awkward, especially with a more mature crowd. The art hanging on the wall lured her over. A lavish impressionist style painting seemed to harmonize with the quartet's musical tones. Next to it hung a large weaving. She admired the creative expression of multi-media textures and materials creating intricate yet powerful abstract forms.

"There you are," said Mara. "Enjoying yourself?"

"Absolutely. I love your art collection."

"Yes, that's a nice piece." She sipped her bubbly drink. "I'm an artist as well."

"Oh, what is your work like?"

She smiled and tugged on her necklace. "You could say I'm more of a conceptual artist. But similar to the weaver, I do like to pull strings." She glanced about for a moment. "Come with me, I have something for you." She led Cyndra to one of the guest rooms.

They entered and Mara closed the door behind them. "It's good to escape from the crowd, and get to know each other a little better." She sat in a cozy chair and gestured Cyndra to sit on the bed alongside a stack of gift boxes. "You may not know this, but Griff and I are committed environmentalists, and we love donating to organizations and individuals who are making this planet a better place."

Cyndra nodded in agreement. "That's so wonderful of you. Emilio said you were both really good and generous people. He loves taking pictures for you."

"Emilio is so helpful, and you're both doing really good work at Elysium. Tell me, how was your day? What did you learn?" Mara asked with eyebrows lifted.

Cyndra recounted learning all about honey; how it was so beneficial, as well as some being potentially deadly.

"Sounds like Daemon enjoys honey."

"He's obsessed with it. He has some every day in a smoothie."

"That's good to know... I mean, that he's taking care of himself." Her voice softened. "And I hope he's taking good care of you. I know you're getting school credit, but in addition to that, how much is Daemon paying you, if you don't mind me asking." She downed some more of her champagne cocktail.

"Nothing, but I'm learning a lot. It seems fair."

"Nonsense!" insisted Mara as she sat up, with a little effort, in a chair she kept sinking into. "All the hard work you do for him, benefiting him for free. What are you expected to live on? Men; all they are really concerned about is financial accumulation and random fornication."

Cyndra's lips pressed together from Mara's colorful language. She took a breath, then considered this different perspective on what she was worth at Elysium Jungle. "I could use some extra spending money."

"Of course, you can," she said, lifting her hand.

"Cyndra, I want to show my gratitude for all you do at Daemon's." Mara pointed to the stack of boxes.

Cyndra opened a small package, revealing four bottles of essential oil; jasmine, orange blossom, rose and ylang ylang. "Oh my gosh, these are my favorites." Taking a long inhale of each of the precious oils, her eyes rolled back in her head, and she released an ahh.

"I heard you like aromatherapy, and these are the real deal, not adulterated. Use them wisely, they're like gold." Mara pointed to the next box.

Cyndra opened the gift to find Morpheus, Energeia, and Eros Nectars, five bottles of each.

"I don't know how much Daemon gives out free samples, but I'm sure you could use plenty of these nectars. The way you work, you need to both keep up your energy and be able to relax, or you'll burn out." She took another sip of her bubbly drink.

"They're wonderful," she said, brushing her hand through her hair.

"If I don't give you meaningful gifts, who will?" Mara's gaze shifted to the last three boxes, which were larger.

Cyndra opened one to find a red lace mini dress exhibiting delicate design. It included elongated heart shaped hair clips, and matching shoes. She stood up and held the dress over her body. "Looks like a perfect fit." The second box contained a dress with an exotic leopard print. She tore open the last box, uncovering another mini dress; a revealing black fish-net mesh that captured her imagination. Glossy black, dart shaped hair clips accessorized it along with shoes. "Oh, I'm so grateful to you Mara, you're the most kind and generous person I've ever met." Cyndra leaned over and gave her a hug.

"Women know what other women like; something new to accent your beauty." She gently tugged at the bottom of her necklace which went down between her breasts. "Cyndra, you have been gifted with stunning beauty. You could benefit from that gift. Look at professional athletes. They're taking advantage of the bodies they've been blessed with, and making millions of dollars, right?"

Cyndra nodded in agreement.

"I don't know what you and Daemon do during your time off at night, but if there's an opportunity in life, don't let it go to waste. Whether it's just for pure enjoyment, or for more tangible assets, allow yourself the freedom to explore what's possible."

Cyndra sat still, and pondered those words. *Perhaps Mara offered good advice, after all, look at her success.*

"One final thing. Is Daemon still claiming he has not yet developed the Utopia Nectar?"

"That's right, he's still doing research, it's always on his mind."

"Oh, he makes me crazy. He already has the Utopia Nectar. It's all just part of a big charade to get more money," she said and repositioned herself in her seat. "I'm with Psi-Matics Global, we're purchasing Gaia, the company that funds Daemon. We've discovered what's been going on behind the scenes."

"Are you sure Daemon is not telling the truth?"

"I know it's difficult to accept, but we have the evidence. Daemon doesn't know it yet, but it will all come out once the merger is complete next week. His backup plan is probably to go to another company with Utopia, but we now have a patent on it. Over the last few years, Gaia Nootropics had already paid Daemon more than enough for that nectar product with the so-called research funding. We're going to get it out on the market without any more excessive spending; he's going to have to face reality."

"Wow, that's a lot to take in." She placed her hand on her forehead. "If Utopia Nectar has already been produced, what's it like?"

"I took the opportunity to sample it, although it was just a prototype. Actually, I have to hand it to Daemon, it was quite spectacular. I felt like a goddess, and it lasted several days. Oddly enough, the moon seems to enhance the experience. I can acquire some if you like, even though it's still in the developmental stage." She finished her drink. "One other thing, the taste is terrible. Be sure to have something to wash it down."

"That's okay. I'd love to try it."

"I wouldn't mention this to Daemon if I were you, it will only create a huge argument."

Cyndra carried the boxes in a large gift bag as she and Mara exited the room. They approached Griff, talking to another man.

"Brad Johnson, this is Cyndra Faye, she works next door at the botanical garden," said Mara.

"Nice to meet you," Brad said, shaking her hand. "Griff just gave me some of the nectars you produce there. Good for stamina."

"Remember, it's natural, so it's okay to use all you

want, right Cyndra?" said Griff.

"They are natural, but strong. You might want to be careful," she replied.

"Brad knows what he wants and goes for it, right?" Griff said, giving him a gentle elbow to the side.

"You got that right. Thanks again for everything," Brad said, and exited with his bag full of bottled mojo.

On her way home after the party, Cyndra's mind spun with all she had experienced; the gifts she received from Mara, and their lavish home. As she walked up to her front door, a huge moth flew around her porch light. It dwarfed all the usual moths and bugs. Because of its size it reminded Cyndra of a bird, or a bat, but its wings beat so fast they were a blur, making a deep buzzy sound. As it zoomed around the light, she opened the door quickly, and shut it directly behind her. It elevated her heartbeat, but once inside she took a deep breath, and softened. She got on social media, letting freinds know she was rubbing shoulders with the elite, and posted some pictures from the party. Later, she enjoyed snuggling with her adorable roommate.

"Nisha, you're such a beautiful cat." Her hand slid down the velvety black fur. Nisha's big yellow eyes closed halfway. "Do you think I would look irresistible in this red dress?" She held it up proudly. Nisha swished her tail a few times. "I'll take that as a yes."

Cyndra put away her gifts. Her mind swirled with thoughts of Mara; and the challenging ideas about Daemon. Was she telling the truth about Daemon? If not, why would she lie? Perhaps he really was creating an illusion about Utopia. Maybe he actually did need more money. She finally realized she had no idea of any of the financials or any other details, and so just let it all go. Mara's suggestion about sex with Daemon surprised her, although it had already been a fantasy. Cyndra considered physical intimacy with Daemon, and even though there was some age difference, why not? *We're both mature adults, making our own decisions.*

She looked at the moon through the window. It was about halfway to being full. She had desires, and for too long pretended they didn't exist. Why not be more carefree and indulge herself once and a while? He was attractive and non-threatening. Her heart beat quickened, and her legs tingled. Cyndra was unsure about some aspects of herself, but was confident about her pleasing appearance. She delved into luscious fantasies of what she would say to him and how she would act. Driving Daemon out of his logical mind felt quite seductive.

As she relaxed more deeply into the couch, Daemon's image dissolved into the magnetic moonlight bathing her space. The ensemble of night insects became more apparent. Toads added their strong rhythmic beats. Nisha's ears twitched. The organic, musical sound further quieted Cyndra's mind. There was no need for any activity at this time, and her body became gently immobilized. The anesthesia of sleep covered her like a soft blanket. Despite the need for deep restorative sleep, she only slept lightly on the couch, going in and out of fragmented dreams. She laid there the rest of the night, with Nisha watching over her.

Mara and Griff were winding down from the party,

alone in their large quiet house. "It looks like we got a good genetic sample from Cyndra's straw," Griff said. "Combined with the electromagnetic signature, it'll improve her connection to the psychotronic beam.

"You got her technologically, and I got her emotionally," said Mara. "That's the beauty of teamwork."

"It's just a matter of time," Griff said.

"How's the psychotronic device doing?" she asked.

"I haven't checked it today, let's go up and see if there's any improvement."

Inside the psychotronic room, Griff pressed the power button and looked at the information coming up on the screen. "Looks like we're still getting interference with the signal. The beam was pretty stable up until a few days ago. Emilio said that was when they spread rock powders in the garden. The Shungite they used could be causing the problem. Anyway, we'll need an amplifier in Cyndra's house to boost the signal."

"Okay, we should hide it inside something she adores, so it will be well cared for... I think I know just the thing. I'll contact Dr. Lev's team about creating it." She took a sip of champagne. "Technology is such a gift... and with Cyndra, it's going to be the gift that keeps giving."

Day Six

"Control thy passions lest they take vengeance on thee."
Epictetus

Daemon's meditation room window framed red bands of light radiating up from the horizon into the early morning sky. Below this brilliant display, marsh rabbits enjoyed a breakfast of clover fern and gotu kola. After his meditation, he consumed a cup of Brazilian ginseng tea, inviting a surge of energy through his veins. Positive that real progress would be made in his efforts, he imagined and felt events unfolding in a beneficial way. He looked forward to Cyndra's visit tonight. Just the thought of her doubled the vital action of the ginseng.

"Good morning, Cyndra, time to wake up," Daemon called out as he both knocked on her door and looked through the window. The blinds were left open, and he could easily see her stretched out on the couch. She quivered a little, then jumped up and opened the door.

Her hand shaded squinting eyes. "I think you show up earlier and earlier each day." Her kitty sat on the floor, next to Cyndra's bare feet. Nisha's eyes mirrored the sun, as she stared intently at Daemon.

"I hope the couch offered you a good night's sleep, because there's plenty of harvesting to do," Daemon said.

"Can you give me half an hour?" she said, pulling her

hair back, trying to look more presentable.

"Ok, but you owe me one. Remember that tonight." He strutted off to his house for another cup of tea.

The morning warmed up as Daemon and Cyndra hunted plants. They searched an area where the dream garden bordered Eros, the garden of passions. Here grew the legendary mandrake, whose fruit induced sensuous dreams.

"There they are," Daemon said with a big smile.

Cyndra quietly observed Daemon's excitement, yet she did not seem too impressed. The plants stood barely a foot tall, with scraggly leaves. The small fruits resembled tiny yellow tomatoes. She squatted down, plucked the highly touted dream fruit and tossed them in a small bag. Her clothes were becoming moist with sweat.

"Just being around these little devils gets you hot and sweaty, doesn't it?" he joked.

"How many of these are *you* going to need?" Cyndra asked, while hunting the berry-like psychotropics. "This bag is half full."

"That's more than enough."

Before getting up, she noticed an odd shaped thing on the ground, like some type of large insect or larvae. "What's that?"

"It looks like a cocoon." Daemon reached down, picked it up and placed it in another bag. "I'll take it back and see what it becomes." He looked around, getting his bearings. "It's time to visit an Australian Christmas Tree."

"I love the smell of Christmas trees."

"This isn't what you think it is. It gets its name because it blooms during Christmas."

The Australian Christmas Tree, Nuytsia floribunda, native to Australia, was the largest parasitic plant in the world, standing thirty feet tall. With roots extending 500 feet, and feeding on almost all types of plants, it offered plenty of potential to create interesting combinations of mind enhancing constituents.

"Oh my gosh, look at those flowers!" Cyndra fell in love with the large, abundant clusters of deep yellow flowers. "Hey, wait a minute. I thought you said it blooms during Christmas?"

"The plant blooms at the beginning of summer. Remember the seasons are reversed down under, December is summer."

"Okay, just seems odd to have Christmas when it's hot."

"Collect some flowers, they're good for meditation."

Cyndra snipped, reached and climbed. She hung onto the lower branches to grab the floral delicacies, and filled a large bag.

Several weeks ago, Daemon had cut away a swathe of bark, and now sticky sap oozed from the tree's wound. Swooshing away some bees, he scraped off the sap with a knife and placed it in a jar. "I can make this into a wonderful syrup for the mandrake. An Aussie style Dream Time Dessert."

Finishing with the sticky condiment, he faced Cyndra, and cradled her hand in his. Her azure eyes filled his mind. "I just want to make sure you're okay with getting together tonight. Just a relaxed vibe. Think of it as cultivating emotional intelligence."

Cyndra nodded in agreement. "I don't have any expectations for tonight. I trust we'll have a memorable evening, no matter what happens." She winked at Daemon.

That simple gesture nourished a neglected part of Daemon. Although a seeker of greater consciousness, tonight he may simply become more care free and indulgent. "It's an opportunity to get to know each other better, and unwind. You've been working hard; don't want you to get burned out." He laid his hand on her shoulder.

"I'll remember that next time you ask me to move tons of dirt or chop down a forest." She playfully brushed his hand off.

As they walked back to the lab, there was a shed snake skin stretched across the path. Carefully pulling the fragile, paper-like molt from around bushes and other plants, Daemon kept it intact. As he gathered it all up, he realized its incredible length, and carried it back to be measured.

Arriving at the lab, they found Katashi and Shavonda testing samples.

"How's the research going?" Daemon asked.

Katashi tapped the keyboard and brought up a file. "Last year at Gaia, we had analyzed the neurological effects from some of the extracts you sent to us back then. Now, I'm comparing that with your recent extracts from the same plant species. Quite a difference."

Daemon sat the rolled up shed skin on the table. "Do you know what kind of snake produced this?" he asked Shavonda.

Shavonda tilted her head, getting different perspectives. There was no trace of a pattern, and the scales were smooth not keeled. Of course, she considered its large size. "If it's a native species, it must be an indigo snake."

"Yes, I caught a glimpse of one a month ago. Armando's seen it too."

The eastern indigo snake, *Drymarchon couperi*, was the largest native non-venomous snake in the United States, with a record length just over nine feet. Glossy black with an indigo blue iridescence, it also exhibited red coloration on its lower jaw and throat. When threatened, it hissed loudly and vibrated its tail resembling a rattlesnake.

They straightened out the ephemeral skin on the counter and measured it. "Wow, this snake is about ten feet. That's a record," said Daemon.

"It must be well fed," said Katashi.

Daemon rolled up the skin, put it aside, and returned to investigating Utopia. They analyzed the results from the latest extracts. Daemon observed the results on the computer. Completely absorbed in exploring the chemical contents, his gaze grew brighter. It was becoming better than getting lost in online videos.

Late in the day, Daemon and Azarias sipped ginger tea on the lanai, gazing out into his well-crafted, yet mysterious verdant world. Amidst this green palate, a hibiscus bush poured open its flamboyant, scarlet petals. Acacia flowers sweetened the air, and crows echoed in the distance. Despite the serene setting, Daemon's face was drawn.

Azarias spoke up, "I see one of your toads has decided to come out during the day." He pointed to an area of ground at the edge of the hibiscus bush.

"That's weird," Daemon said. Although he enjoyed the mind altering chemicals that the toads brought to his garden, he missed the small reptiles and amphibians that they gobbled up at night. Now, it seemed they may be consuming the daytime critters as well.

"There's another one," Azarias pointed out, looking toward the other side.

"I hope this is not a trend," Daemon said, folding his arms. He didn't mind the abundance of toads as long as they were hidden during the day. But, if more visible, he imagined complaints from visitors and environmentalists.

"Maybe it's indicative of an energetic shift from darkness to light?" said Azarias, sipping some of his hot, spicy beverage.

"Or else, the darkness has become so empowered that it intrudes upon the light." After stating this, Daemon immediately recognized the negative nature of his mind, and made a point of seeing a more positive outlook, like his mentor. He noticed the benefit of his mindfulness meditation practice, becoming more aware of his thought patterns.

A huge grasshopper, sporting red wings and a golden yellow body, crawled on the ground in front of the toad.

In an instant, the toad's tongue lashed out as its mouth lunged onto the grasshopper. Strong jaws held the insect as its legs kicked to no avail, and it completely disappeared in a few chomps. The southeastern lubber grasshopper, *Romalea microptera,* one of the largest native grasshoppers, commanded a special niche in the garden. It sequestered toxins from over 50 plant species, making it too poisonous for any predator to consume… until now.

"I can't believe something is actually eating a lubber grasshopper," said Daemon. "Finally, a predator to recycle those guys into the system."

Azarias shifted his gaze back to Daemon. "How's the research into Utopia Nectar?"

"Good. Just got some new equipment to help analyze the extracts."

Azarias embodied the fantastic potential that naturally resides within humanity. Ultimately, all technology represented the externalized form of our own internal power and abilities. Logic and analysis were important aspects of mind, but the quest for Utopian Nectar went beyond that. "In addition to the machines, utilize the alchemical elements," said Azarias. "Choose fire to energize and transform your search."

In alchemy, the element fire purified and activated whatever you added to it. Fire not only assisted positive, light filled endeavors, but could also strengthen any state of mind. To use the fire element safely required a clear intent regarding one's thoughts and actions.

Daemon closed his eyes for a moment, inviting a deep internalization of his mentor's teachings. He carried plenty of the fire energy in the form of passion for his work. Along with that he possessed a luscious passion for Cyndra. He tried to keep his feelings for her separate from the search for Utopia, but with little success. "Cyndra is coming over tonight. I'm attracted to her, but considering our roles as teacher and student, it seems inappropriate."

"Take that passion for her, and channel it as inspiration for your goal."

"I'll do what I can." Daemon finished his tea. "Still planning on being here tomorrow night for the fire ceremony?"

"Yes." He leaned in closer. "Be cautious, fire illuminates and empowers not only what you desire, but also what you dread."

Cyndra stood naked in front of her mirror, caressing her body with essential oils. The orange blossom and jasmine expressed their hypnotic potential on her fresh, smooth skin. She imagined that it could simmer Daemon's brain, burning away the extraneous logic, leaving only red hot embers of desire. Her hips swayed involuntarily to her favorite gothic music. Without putting on any undergarments, she slid into her crimson lace mini dress from Mara. It hugged her slender frame, accenting subtle curves, as if made just for her. She clipped the heart shaped hair pins with pointy ends into her blonde locks. Daemon might be a know it all, but she was going to school him tonight. Her eyes flashed an electric blue, and her hot pink lips glimmered as she smiled.

"Am I the cat's meow?" she asked Nisha, who responded by licking her chops. Cyndra stroked her fur, grateful for the confirmation. She got a head start on the evening by taking some of the Eros and Morpheus Nectars that Mara had given her. A giddiness resonated through her, with an elevated heart beat and humming nervous system. Stepping outside, the flutter of wings surrounded her. The bat sized moths dived and circled as if Cyndra had become their new source of light.

"It sounds like you guys are really buzzed," she said and smiled. One of them hovered in front of her, extending its proboscis. Tickling her neck, the sensation rippled down her spine, and she picked up her pace.

Daemon answered the door to find Cyndra with her two fuzzy friends floating around her. She swooshed them away and dashed into his house with the door shutting immediately behind her.

"Welcome," said Daemon, and for a moment, his mouth hung open. Trying to compose himself he said, "That's an incredible dress; you look amazing." His entire face was smiling. "And what's up with the moths? I suppose even the garden inhabitants find you irresistible."

"It's just another night in your crazy jungle world," she said nonchalantly, and tussled her hair back.

"Maybe they're drawn to your sweet aura." He leaned toward her and inhaled deeply. His eyes closed as Cyndra's scent swirled through his brain and tingles ran deep down in his body, triggering an energetic boost. "Your fragrance is so uplifting, in many ways," he said with a wink, then gestured toward the dining room. "Make yourself comfortable, have a drink."

They sat together in a soft, warm glow, as dozens of candles flickered all over the room. World music filled the space with tribal beats and exotic sounds. Daemon handed her a bottle of Eros Nectar, and she promptly indulged in his potion. Her tongue glistened with three droppers full of the sweet serum. Not to be outdone, Daemon took the same amount. He offered her some of the mandrake fruit they collected earlier. "Notice the aroma of the fruit. It's a complex blend of over 50 constituents. The scent alone can be mind-altering."

"I think you're the one that needs the mental alteration," she said. Before her sat a bowl filled with cherry sized, yellow fruit shimmering with syrup. She spooned one out, and held it to her nose. "Smells like apples, hmm… but with melon and berries." She placed it in her mouth, and savored the coveted nootropic. "This is the best mandrake fruit I've ever had," she said and smiled. Her eyelids lowered halfway. "See how happy my taste buds are." She slid her sweetly glazed tongue out of her mouth.

They continued to enjoy a light hearted conversation, and finished off the dreamy dessert. Daemon began to loosen up under the influence of his love goddess nectar. "You're going to dream your little ass off tonight."

"Don't you worry about my dreamy little ass." She inserted the Eros dropper into her mouth and sucked out the sublime fluid. Then her tongue slid across her lips. "I'm really buzzed."

"I guess so, you've had enough to make one of those

old drones at El Dorado stay up all night long." Daemon stared at her for a while. She seemed to become more radiant and alluring by the minute. "Careful you don't overdo it."

Cyndra feigned a pout, then scanned the room. "What are those pictures on the wall?" she asked. They got up and walked over for a closer look. There were a couple of framed photos of white buildings and islands surrounded by a cobalt blue sea and sky.

"Those were taken during a couple of trips to Greece when I was a child," Daemon explained.

"Looks so beautiful. Are you going to visit again?"

"Who knows, the way things are going, I can't think about travel now." His hand brushed the back of his neck.

"Oh, look at that vase."

An ancient Greek vase sat on a credenza. It had a golden glaze, with graceful, stylized figures silhouetted in black along with a black coiled serpent, and bordered with decorative lines and dots. Nearby was a stack of papers; printouts on nootropics from his never ending research.

"I value my heritage." He supported his hands on his hips. "Especially the Golden Age of Greece. So much creative genius."

"When you work me in the garden, looks like you've inherited some of that know how. Like, you know how to make me hot and sweaty." She gave him a wink.

Daemon's expression brightened. "Watch out, that work in the garden was just a warm up. I can make you aware of muscles you didn't know you had."

"Oh really? If I had my way, you wouldn't be able to move a muscle."

A techno dance vibe mixed into the music. Cyndra began to sway with the beat. Daemon shadowed her movements. "You move so gracefully," he said as they began to dance.

Cyndra's hips buoyed up and down, moving easily from the elastic strength of her long, toned legs. Her mini dress hiked up her thighs. Daemon's energy rose, his hips bobbed in sync with the beat. She twisted and reeled, with a spine like a snake. Daemon found a more percussive rhythm, stepping, hopping, and rebounding energy up through his whole body. They weaved a kinesthetic spell of attraction on each other, and their gaze locked. Cyndra's eyes deepened to indigo blue, and Daemon's smoldered black as thunder. As the tempo increased, they frolicked with passion. Cyndra's body moistened from the elevated vigor.

"Could you turn up the ceiling fans?" she asked.

The increased air flow further liberated Cyndra's movement; she dove deep into bending and transforming her shape. The candlelight twinkled and strobed under the fan's breeze. Her straw colored hair swished and flowed like a wild aura. Riding up her hips, her dress barely covered the treasured foundation of her feminine form. Daemon throbbed from the base of his spine to his brain. The beat quickened, and they stoked themselves into a trance state. Their hearts pulsed in time with the music and each other.

BEEP! BEEP! BEEP!

"What's that?" Cyndra screeched.

"It's the fire alarm," Daemon replied. The fans had blown some of his papers into the candles, and he rushed over to put them out. He turned off the fans, music, and the alarm, but the alarm wouldn't stop. It kept beeping. Retrieving some tools from his garage, he stepped onto a chair and disconnected the annoying device. It continued to sound off, fueled by an internal battery. Frustrated, he grabbed a hammer and smashed it until the blaring stopped.

Cyndra adjusted her hair pins and straightened out her dress. Daemon wiped his brow and took a deep breath. They stood still. The remaining ecstatic energy quietly dissipated through their bodies. The spell seemed to be broken.

"I guess it's getting late," Cyndra said, her eyebrows raised in a questioning gesture.

"Sure," said Daemon, "we have a big day tomorrow." He walked Cyndra back to her house. The half-moon was especially bright. The toads reverberated with their drum-like call. The scent of moon flowers harmonized with Cyndra's fragrant oils. Her porch light attracted only the small, native moths and bugs. Standing in front of her door, they hugged. Daemon leaned in for a kiss on the lips. Cyndra pulled away.

Daemon immediately spoke up, "Oh, I'm sorry, I thought---"

"Oh no, you're okay Daemon. I just, I don't know…It's my fault. I'm sorry."

"No, no. There's nothing to apologize for. Everything in its own time. Thanks for a fantastic evening. And may your dreams be even more fantastic."

"You too."

As soon as the door shut, she wondered why she refused his kiss. After all, that was what she wanted, wasn't it? Confused, she decided to cool off with a quick shower. Afterwards, there was still a residual sizzle from tonight's encounter. Despite her rebuttal of Daemon's attempt at intimacy, she felt restless, and needed some form of release or distraction. She opened a drawer revealing a smooth, battery operated instrument. Momentarily contemplating the erasing of tension with her little toy, she changed her mind and chose to have something to eat instead. Sitting at the kitchen table, she crunched potato chips followed by sticky, glazed doughnuts. Afterwards, feeling quite satiated and a bit groggy, Cyndra was ready for sleep.

She enjoyed the sensation of floating in a pool at night. Cool, silvery light glazed the surface of the water as her body spread out on a plastic raft. Her cream colored skin glowed, and her hair glistened, like soft fiber optics. Daemon massaged her neck and shoulders while complementing her talents and beautiful body. Cyndra loved being with him.

The raft began to change. It moved and became squirmy, as if it were alive. It's color changed from yellow to grey, and its smooth texture grew bumpy. Her body tightened; her breath shortened. She found herself floating on a mass of buoyant amphibians. She looked to Daemon for help, but instead this only made her heart race faster. His skin grew warty. He continued to massage Cyndra, but his hands and fingers felt slimy and wriggly. His body transformed and split up into chunks, each of them morphing into big lumpy toads.

Noxious chemicals oozed from the creatures, infecting the water, turning it into a psychoactive soup. The moon light brightened and glimmered hypnotically on the wet denizens. The light grew cold, and penetrated her skin with an anesthetizing effect. She couldn't feel her body and lost control. The lunar fluorescence glared deep inside her, freezing her mind. Unable to swim, she sank beneath the surface, going deep into unconsciousness.

After his meditations and review of the day, Daemon began to unwind. Although he wished things would have progressed more with Cyndra, he realized it was enough, like Azarias suggested. Good to take it slow. His breathing relaxed, and his body let go of any contraction. He quietly crawled into bed and fell asleep.

He was naked, laying face up, with Cyndra kneeling next to him. She poured honey on his body, then licked it off. His body perked and quivered with delicious excitement. However, she kept pouring the sweet liquid. More and more, until it completely covered him like lacquer. The viscous substance glued him down; she had completely trapped him. The honey began to crystalize. Daemon found himself encased in a large block of golden crystal, like a prehistoric ant trapped in amber.

Day Seven

"(Elysium)...Bloometh the fair flower of perfect bliss.
And o'er that lovely land fragrance is ever shed, while
they mingle all manner of incense with the far-shining
fire on the altar of the gods. From the other side sluggish
streams of darksome night belch forth a boundless
gloom."
Pindar

The overcast sky hung oppressively like soft lead.
Diffuse light unveiled an unusual stillness in the garden.
Dense, sultry air permeated everything. Daemon
knocked on Cyndra's door. The door cracked open,
barely revealing Cyndra.

"I have a headache," she said, frowning. Nisha
meowed in the background. "Be quiet," she whispered.

"I'm sorry you're not feeling well. How about some
willow bark for your headache?" he asked.

"If you don't mind, I would like to just go to the store
for some normal pain killer, and get Nisha some cat
food. Can I borrow your car or shall I call a ride?"

"Okay, take my car, just to the store and back. When
you feel better there's prep work for the fire ceremony
tonight." He then proceeded to the lab.

Shavonda and Katashi stood near a window as
Daemon entered. They saw something move in the
plants just outside. "It's a toad," she said. I thought they
only came out at night."

Katashi looked closely. "There's another one."

"I see they're out again," said Daemon as he set a bag down on the counter. "Azarias and I saw them yesterday as well. What do you think, Shavonda?"

"Cane toads are known for their behavioral plasticity. Going from nocturnal to diurnal is pretty rare in the animal kingdom, but they can do it. It's called phase shift."

"Why does that happen?" asked Katashi.

"Maybe they can't sleep during the day, like they've got insomnia or something. Who knows what can happen in this dopey world?" Shavonda smiled, and everyone settled down at the lab table.

Daemon reached into the bag. "Besides the toads, we've also got this." He pulled out a jar containing a large moth. "It emerged from its cocoon last night. They've recently appeared around the garden. Looks like a type of sphinx moth."

Shavonda picked up the jar and the moth bounced its wings against the glass. Her eyes locked on it, deciphering the subtle earth tone patterns to reveal its hidden identity. After a few moments she announced, "Manduca occulta, the occult sphinx moth."

"What about those big, yellow spots on its abdomen?" Daemon asked.

"Warning coloration."

The occult sphinx moth fed on toxic plants like angel's trumpets and other nightshades, growing in their native range of Central America. To reach the nectar within the deep trumpet flowers, their proboscis was extremely long, several times the length of their bodies.

111

They received mind altering tropane alkaloids from the nectar, and as caterpillars they acquired alkaloids from the leaves. These creatures were saturated with nightshade compounds, thus the warning colors.

"Last night there were three by my front door, and more outside the lab. What's up?" asked Daemon.

"Moths have sensory organs that aren't well understood. I'm not sure what could attract them," said Shavonda, brushing back her dreads. "It's rare they come to Florida; they're considered a stray species."

Daemon's brow furrowed. "The pupae that we found suggests a generation has grown up here, but we never saw the caterpillars." He looked again at the moth. "Perhaps they were well hidden."

Back to the work at hand, he reviewed the test results from various plant extracts, looking for patterns or any clues to a more expanded consciousness. Keenly aware of the days going by, his gaze narrowed. "I wish Psi-Matics Global wasn't pressuring Gaia so much." He turned toward Katashi. "Have you found out anything else about them?"

"After some research, I've uncovered some suspicious activity, and that's coming from multiple sources." He went on and explained how Psi-Matics Global had taken over other supplement companies, where the products were now having questionable effects. Customers complained of going into trance or hypnotic states. It suggested that they tampered with the products, perhaps using frequency technology, which was undetectable with traditional chemical analysis.

They sat quietly for a moment. Shavonda turned to

Daemon, "On a brighter note, Katashi not only has the dirt on Psi-Matics but also on your garden. Let's see it."

Daemon and Shavonda observed as Katashi tapped his keyboard and pulled up a diagram of the garden. It displayed data on soil fungi and microorganisms, and mapped out their spread over time. Years ago, many blank spaces existed in the plotting, but now the fungi and microorganisms completely filled all areas of soil in Daemon's garden. The mycorrhizal fungi connected to other mushrooms as well as plants. Additionally, the mycorrhizal fungi transported not just minerals and water to the plants, but also psychoactive compounds, similar to the parasitic plants. He noted that the magnetic bacteria blanketed the swampy areas, and monoatomic producing bacteria dominated much of the other areas of the garden.

Shavonda spoke, "We are discovering new alkaloids and other active substances in literally every plant species we test."

Katashi followed up, "The molecular structures of these alkaloids are getting so novel and complex, that the computer programs are having a difficult time calculating their probable effects."

Daemon's eyes sparkled with the news, then his phone rang.

"This is Professor Edwards from Caloosa University. We are doing a routine, unannounced visit to your facility today; in fact, we are pulling into your parking area as we speak."

Daemon's face turned pale as he realized the person they wanted to see, Cyndra, was not here. He immediately called her. There was no answer, only a message that her mailbox was full and could not leave a message. He hastened out to meet them, and to stall for time. They received a tour of the operation; the Sales Center, the tour garden, Daemon's home, and the lab. They repeatedly asked about Cyndra and her living quarters.

Daemon finally acquiesced, and took them to her house. The front window blinds were open and the two gentlemen looked inside. There were cups and dishes with chips and donuts setting out next to her romance novels. Nisha sat on a serving dish left on the kitchen table. Clothes were strewn all over, and a vibrator was visible laying in a half opened drawer. Daemon pretended he was in the process of having another key made, and at the moment didn't have access. He feared going inside and finding something even worse than what was already visible. He explained that Cyndra just left to get some medication. The two gentlemen said they would wait for half an hour. For a while, they wandered through the garden. Daemon continued to call but to no avail. Eventually, time ran out. The visitors had seen enough.

Professor Edwards spoke, "This program is being billed as a world class experience in working with medicinal plants. I would imagine professionalism would prevail throughout, including the upkeep of living quarters, maintaining good communication and proper access." The two began to leave for their car. "Mr. Makarios, I'm sorry to say, this report is not going to be very favorable."

Daemon sulked back toward the lab. His teeth clenched as he wondered about Cyndra, *why didn't she answer, why doesn't she keep up with her messages, and how could she let her place get so messy?* Daemon stopped in his tracks for a moment, and invited his mind to do the same. He realized his part in this event. His behavior, along with the Eros and Morpheus Nectars last night, were connected to all of it. He decided to let go of the anger. What was the worst thing that could happen? What if he lost the Caloosa contract? He held a much higher goal, and from that vantage point, clarity created proper perspective. His gaze was calm and steady. He stepped into the lab, fully present, and ready to return to his exploration into Utopia.

Just as Daemon settled down into his chair, he heard Cyndra return. His calm mood vanished as he ran out and confronted her. "Where have you been? The store is only a few minutes away. You've been gone over an hour," he said harshly as they walked over to her place.

"I got caught in a traffic jam. What's the big deal?" Her hands lifted.

"Caloosa showed up for a surprise inspection, expecting to see you. It didn't go well." His brow furrowed. "You always want to have your phone, and yet when I try to call, I can't reach you," he said.

"Sorry, I accidentally left it on silent."

"Caloosa didn't like the looks of your place," he said, as they entered her living area. "What has happened?" His complexion became inflamed.

"I guess it was the dream herbs. Last night I felt really, um, restless. Things got tossed around. Was planning to clean up later today." Her mouth drooped.

"We may lose the Caloosa account. That's not just a problem for me, but it would ruin your class credits."

"I feel really bad, I promise to do better."

"You need to do better, although it may be too late." Daemon took a deep breath as he tried to calm down. "Check with Armando for your next assignment. I've got work to do." He rushed out and slammed the door.

Insulated inside the lab, Daemon forgot everything else, engulfing himself in research. Together with Shavonda and Katashi, they worked throughout the afternoon.

The late afternoon clouds grew dark. Trees bent and waved in the wind. The lab rumbled from distant thunder. They decided to wrap up the research to avoid any electrical overload from lightning. After everyone else left, Daemon received a call from Mara.

"Just wanted to let you know a friend of ours, Brad Johnson, was hospitalized from using your nectars. He suffered a heart attack, and you will be receiving a summons. Just wanted to give you a heads up and I think you should stop what you are doing. Daemon, your actions are more destructive than you realize."

Daemon held his breath. He sat down slowly, and hung up the phone unconsciously. He reconsidered what he was doing with his work. Is it really what he thinks it is…better for humanity, or is he just fooling himself? He faced the storm outside, silhouetted against strobes of lightning; his mind charged with questions. Thunder shook him to the core. Bolts of electricity scorched the sky, as Daemon's goals clashed with fear and uncertainty. He became one with the booming sound, inviting it to demolish any resistance to his awakening. He found acceptance for chaos. It resonated a deeper octave of truth, that led to a quiet space within, the eye of the storm. He had no choice but to continue his quest.

His phone alerted him to a text. It was from Azarias. *See you tonight at the fire ceremony. Your fascinating insights into nature are a gift to humanity.*

Daemon sighed with appreciation for his mentor. Things happen in life that we don't understand, that we can't control. He didn't even know any details of the man that Mara spoke of. What was his general health; what were all the factors? He also couldn't trust anything Mara said; was it all made up? Daemon's dark mood, like the storm, had lifted and quickly moved on. He arose from his chair smoothly, and trekked toward the heart of his garden, for the impending fire celebration.

The warm liquid light of numerous torches illuminated the winding pathway toward the celebration. At the site, many more of the fiery lamp posts staked out the perimeter of the observance. In the center of the gathering burned a stack of felled trees, including aromatic sandalwood and palo santo. The ceremony bordered a portion of the spawning pool.

The spawning pool, a circular pond, spanned 100 feet in diameter, and marked the center of Daemon's garden. The pool acquired its name from the cane toads that bred there heavily. The entire pond squirmed with the aroused creatures, oozing and adrenalizing the water.

The toads also bred in other waterways throughout the garden, but this spot was their favorite. Water datura, *datura ceratocaula*, grew in the shallows of this body of water, and tadpoles devoured these plants. Like conscientious parents, the toads preferred this nourishing habitat for their slimy offspring.

A tribe of drummers thumped and pounded their djembes, congas and bongos. Maracas and egg shakers seasoned the percussion. Primordial rhythms enlivened the night. Firelight wavered throughout the festival; and coalescing with sound, delineated everyone with a resonating glow. Dancers undulated and flashed their phosphorescent wands and clothing. They pulsed and mirrored the shape of sound, contrasted against the backdrop of a black forest.

Tables laid out an abundance of garden grown food and drink that nourished and blessed the participants. Colorful flowers garnished nootropic teas, juices, and bowls of exotic fruit. Shavonda, Katashi and Armando hovered around the table, sampling the exquisite fare.

Daemon wore a black shirt emblazoned with crimson and orange organic designs, as if reflecting the fire. Cyndra wore her leopard print mini dress. The soft, tawny gold matched her hair, while the strong, black markings mirrored a darkness in her eyes. She stood off to the side hanging out with Emilio.

Azarias wore all white. He and Daemon conversed in the shadows.

"Do what you can to heal your relationship with Cyndra. She's your teacher," said Azarias.

"I thought *you* were my teacher," replied Daemon.

"Actually, teachers are everywhere, but Cyndra is like the tenured professor of your life lessons. I simply provide reminders and reassurance."

Daemon tilted his head and glanced over at Cyndra, still talking to Emilio. He could apologize for being too rough, and he should have inquired about her dreams last night.

"I feel so springy," said one of the dancers that bounded her way over to Daemon and Azarias. Her bare feet moved constantly. "I think I need to chill," she said. "Maybe stepping through that pond will cool me down."

"I don't think so," said Daemon. He explained that the toads released cardiac glycosides, adrenaline, and other agents into the water, and that would energize her even more. "Maybe some tea," he suggested, and gestured toward the table. "Try the passion flower."

The energy of the ceremony rose. The drumming quickened, the volume of the toads increased, the dancers moved more frenetically. Cyndra and Emilio began to dance.

Daemon excused himself from Azarias, and meandered toward Cyndra. He paused near the fire. His skin became hot, and the heat sank deep into his bones. His body swayed and his breathing opened. He wondered what Cyndra saw in Emilio, who seemed so flaky. His work was marginal, and he seemed to be in his own world most of the time. But there they were, dancing and smiling. Daemon didn't recall Cyndra smiling so much while she was dancing with him at his house. His pulse rate increased. He turned to Shavonda, who was beginning to move with the music.

"Would you like to dance?" he asked

"Sure, why not?" she said as they moved into the cleared area, along with Cyndra and Emilio. Shavonda moved beautifully.

While Daemon danced with Shavonda, he paid more attention to Cyndra. Their gaze would meet, and then look away. The drumming became intense, and they kept moving. Daemon and Shavonda edged closer to Cyndra and Emilio, then backed away. They were all beginning to break a sweat.

The drumming shifted gears and slowed down. Cyndra leaned into Emilio and spoke to him. He stopped dancing and stepped away. Shavonda returned to the refreshments. Cyndra looked directly into Daemon's eyes. They approached each other, and his hands clasped hers while leaning in and whispering in her ear, "I'm sorry I was so hard on you earlier. Please forgive me."

Cyndra's face softened. "Thanks, it's okay."

Daemon sighed, "I'm glad to hear that."

"Would you like to move a little? I feel like I'm just getting warmed up." She signaled the drummers to crank it up. Her stealthy movement made the leopard print an appropriate choice. Graceful and energetic, she mesmerized Daemon. Her entire body was articulate; every muscle was online. Her taught, slender form revealed an enticing expression of life, with a touch of hunter energy, an element of risk.

"I could watch you dance all night," said Daemon, as he pumped movement through his body. "You are the physical embodiment of enchantment." As he danced, the earth energy of the garden sparkled through his feet and legs. He kept his attention on Cyndra, and noticed her snug outfit inching up her thighs as it was prone to do. "It's good to be seeing so much of you again." It became apparent she wore nothing underneath the dress but scintillating flesh.

Her body perspired in the thick, sensuous night air. The sheer fabric of her attire clutched her torso and became exceedingly translucent. All of her subtle curves and exquisite forms undulated more visibly than ever. She paused for a moment, directly facing Daemon, eyeing him like a target. Without warning, she jumped up onto him, like a predator pouncing on its prey. The front of her body pounded onto his, and held firmly against him. Cyndra's legs wrapped around Daemon's hips and lower back, while her hands held onto his shoulders. Looking into his eyes, she snarled like a wild cat. Releasing her hands, her upper body fell back and downward. She continued to hang on with her legs while her head dangled below his knees. Swaying wave-like, her hands lightly brushed the ground. He looked down at her, and from his vantage point, she completely exposed her most precious kitty anatomy. Daemon's energy expanded into a more euphoric state.

Cyndra pressed her palms into the ground, finding plenty of support. She unlocked her legs, maneuvered them off of Daemon, and extended them up and over her torso, shifting into a hand stand. Moments later, her feet came down to earth as she folded into a standing forward bend. She then propelled herself to an upright position. "I need a drink," she said, fluffing her hair back.

121

Wide eyed, Daemon stood breathless in the presence of such athletic grace and beauty.

Sipping iced herbal teas, they strolled to a more quiet corner of the group event. The percussion slowed and stopped for a break. The rhythm of the toads replaced the drums.

"Cyndra, you're the most captivating woman I've ever known." He stood close, resonating with magnetic attraction towards her. "Tell me more about your dreams, especially last night."

Cyndra recounted being frightened, and how Daemon transformed into toads. As she spoke, several large moths buzzed around her. They tickled her arms and legs as they hovered and skimmed her form.

"They're attracted to your essential oils," said Daemon.

"Haven't you noticed? I'm not wearing any tonight."

"Well, I wasn't aware of any, but I thought there might be a trace or something to draw them."

"Nope. Just me."

"Interesting." Daemon returned to the dream. "It sounds like an inner journey; very deep."

"Increasing self-knowledge sounds good; wish it wasn't so scary."

"Ultimately, it gets easier and better," he reassured her. "It also depends on your perspective on life, and what you really want."

"I thought it was this. I mean, learning about plants, essential oils, and all that. I've gotten a lot out of being here, but now... I don't know. It feels like I am being pulled in opposite directions. Things just don't seem to be what I thought they were. Maybe Mara was right."

"Mara? Do you mean Mara Blackstone?" Daemon asked, his face hardened. "You've spoken to her?"

"Yes, she invited me over to a little party. I wasn't supposed to say anything but...she said you've already created Utopian Nectar."

"What? That's crazy. It's so wrong. How does she even claim to think that?"

"She said she's with Psi-Matics Global, and knows what's happening on the inside with Gaia Nootropics."

Mara is with Psi-Matics Global? Are you kidding? And she has been keeping that from me all this time? What a witch."

That's the company that funds you, isn't it?"

"Yes, they're purchasing the company that funds me. But I can assure you, I have not created Utopia Nectar. What kind of poison has she been putting into your mind?

Daemon attempted to make sense of the situation. *Why was Mara here? To derail his efforts toward Utopia?* He had heard that Emilio was taking pictures of the garden for Mara. *Was this her way of spying on him?*

Daemon yelled at Emilio to come over. As he came close, Daemon spoke up, "Mara Blackstone is undermining Elysium Jungle, and you're working for her."

"It's just odd jobs here and there," Emilio explained.

"I can't keep an employee who works for her in any capacity."

"I'm not hurting anyone."

Daemon's voice became more insistent. "You can't stay here."

"What did I do?"

Daemon roared, "You're fired. Now leave."

Emilio slunk away and left.

Cyndra's mouth hung open as her friend plodded away. "Emilio doesn't deserve that, he's a really good guy."

"Oh please." Daemon shook his head. "And, while you're working here, I don't want you visiting her either."

"That's ridiculous, she's a wonderful and generous woman. Way more generous than you. She supports me with things I like, such as this dress."

"You're here to learn, not to collect gifts."

"Well then, why don't you teach me what I signed up for? As it turns out, I'm just a servant for your own personal interests."

"You know my situation."

"All too well." She stomped off, leaving the combustion filled event.

"Oh crap," Daemon muttered, as he returned to Azarias.

"What was that about?" Azarias inquired.

"Cyndra has some perspectives I don't understand." He brushed his forehead. "How can she be fond of an infuriating woman like Mara Blackstone?"

Azarias stood still, his eyes became intense. "Do you mean Mara and Griff Blackstone?"

"Exactly, do you know them?"

"Yes, they associated with your parents when you were a very young child. How do you know them?"

"Oh my God, my parents hung out with them? Daemon looked confused. "The Blackstones moved into El Dorado next door, I met them on my garden tour. Mara's with Psi-Matics Global, buying out Gaia." Daemon's face turned pale. "Essentially, she's going to be my new boss."

"They were with your parents at the Masonic Lodge," said Azarias.

Daemon froze with apprehension. "Somehow, that doesn't sound good."

"No, it's not a pretty story." Azarias shimmered with a jack-o'-lantern glow from the fire, as he revealed a dark secret that he had kept for perhaps too long. He explained that Mara and Griff used to winter in Tampa many years ago. They excelled in the Masonic Order more than Daemon's parents, Hector and Krysta, and they had convinced his parents to entertain their questionable practices.

"I'm almost afraid to ask, what did my parents do?" Firelight wavered across his face.

Azarias continued, recounting his understanding of what occurred. He had heard that Mara and Griff led rituals performed on Daemon when he was two or three years old. They administered scopolamine, and programmed his mind. Although Azarias was not sure of their desired outcome, he knew Mara had a long standing interest in portals and vortex energy. They possibly conditioned Daemon to create a portal, based on ecology and natural elements. This was reminiscent of Atlantis, where earth energies were concentrated and manipulated in order to rule others. The layout of Elysium Jungle even resembled a well-known illustration of Atlantis, in terms of concentric rings of water and land. As it turned out, Daemon created a garden more magical than he realized, and with Mara eager to claim it as her own.

The fire burned down to embers. The blaze shifted to a red glow. Daemon became queasy, not knowing what to do or think. Standing still and quiet, he let it sink in, like the heat from the fire. He spoke in a hushed tone, "Mara, Griff, my parents, they're all Illuminati, aren't they?"

Azarias nodded.

"So, what does that make me?" He considered the extreme discipline and denial he suffered as a child, and finally recognized it as a form of trauma based mind control. His obsessive research into the illuminati made more sense. He understood them, he was wired like them. Staring deeply into the hot coals, his face glowed a radiant scarlet. Despite the shocking news, his spirit opened even more to his natural and deeply mysterious world. He spoke more boldly, "I created Elysium from my sweat and blood, it is my offspring. Anyone trying to take it away will invoke the part of me that's best left unseen."

Day Eight

"Those who aim at great deeds must also suffer greatly."
Aristotle

Golden shafts of light penetrated the canopy of the tour garden. A red tailed hawk screamed its shrill call, as if to give fair warning to all potential prey of its deadly presence.

The attendance was higher than usual. Mara made a return visit, and Daemon spoke privately with her before the tour. "How dare you show up on my property after all you've done," Daemon said, trying to control the volume of his voice.

"If everything goes as planned, it will soon be my property," she said.

"I can assure you that will never happen," his eyes narrowed, "no matter how much you re-interpret contracts and fine print." Daemon's veins pressed out on his forehead, and he took a few deep breaths to calm down. "Mara, I understand the part you play in life. You remind us how we should *not* act."

"And the role *you've* acted is, I believe, about to run out."

He looked at the time. "I've got a tour to do."

"Relax, this is probably my last visit." She took a drink from her cannister. "With that in mind, I would like to make it quite memorable."

As they moved through Eros, the love garden, Daemon pointed out the grey green foliage of Hawaiian Sandalwood trees. The visitors smiled as an exquisite scent from crimson flowers wafted around them. Bees and butterflies floated between the branches. "The leaves are an aphrodisiac and used in Eros Nectar," said Daemon.

Rubywood, a host tree for the sandalwood, grew close by. It was also an aphrodisiac. The Hawaiian Sandalwood drew out the Rubywood's love inducing chemistry, and combined it with its own, thus enhancing the sandalwood's seductive quality.

"Does Eros Nectar promote promiscuity?" asked Mara. "I understand you were dancing with your employees last night, and very provocatively." She patted her moist forehead with a folded handkerchief. A murmur spread across the crowd.

"Absolutely not," Daemon said resolutely.

"I saw some online posts with dancers and a bonfire. It looked like some enactment of lewd rites."

"Nothing of the sort. It was simply friends and employees getting together after work." Daemon gazed across the crowd. "Let's all stay present, and focused on the plants."

Mara sneered and looked away, and when she did, something caught her attention. She repositioned closer to the edge of the path. Something moved around the base of some butterfly ginger plants. "It's a cane toad. And look, there's another one," she said, pointing her finger. "They're as big as sewer rats."

Everyone stared and gasped at the unwelcome

inhabitants hopping through the garden. Their warty, wrinkly skin epitomized toxicity.

"Look out, they're poisonous," a woman said, as she backed away.

"Please, don't worry, they're harmless," Daemon pleaded.

"Don't be ridiculous, some localities have a bounty on them," said Mara, taking pictures and encouraging her friends to do the same. She turned her head toward a squealing chirp, and moved stealthily in that direction, tracking it to its source. Looking down, she spied the site of a ground nesting bird. A cane toad had invaded the nest, and was feeding on the young birds. Covered in plumage, but not yet able to fly, they hopped and wobbled in their exposed nursery. Mara crouched down, and got the mother lode of film footage. The toad lunged and scooped up another baby chick into its mouth. The main body of the bird lodged inside the toad's mouth, while its wings and legs extended out, frantically shaking. Muffled chirps came from inside the toad's mouth. A few more gulps, and it swallowed the entire bird.

Another toad approached, crunching and devouring the last unfortunate bird. The grey and white feathered parents swooped overhead with high pitched chattering. Although helpless to stop the carnage, they nevertheless signaled urgency to the rest of the environment. After taking plenty of photos and video of the tragic event, she texted some images of the adult birds to her contact at Caloosa for identification. Mara stood up. "The toads are eating Florida's precious wildlife."

Daemon tried to neutralize the outrage. "Don't worry, it's how nature works to maintain balance; there's an abundance of life here. To the Greeks, Elysium was a land of rebirth."

"No, Elysium is the land of the dead," said Mara. She turned to the people gathered around her, and lowered her voice. "I need to go now, remember the plan." With that said, she left the tour, and strode towards her car.

She sped her black SUV out of Elysium Jungle, rumbled down the road for a moment, and then pulled into Elysium's private drive. She followed the narrow, concrete paved road past Daemon's house, then the lab, and turned to park at Cyndra's house. Mara grabbed her gift for Cyndra, including a card. Carrying the soft, black present in her arm, she knew Cyndra would adore it.

Following a pathway bordered by small bushes and herbaceous plants, she advanced toward Cyndra's house. Stretched across the walkway ahead of her lay a thick, black, cylindrical form. It was the diameter of her arm, and as she watched, it began to move. Realizing it was a snake, she immediately froze. Her face paled as her skin grew clammy. The visible section of it stretched over three feet long. Judging from what she could see, this snake dwarfed anything else she had ever seen outside. Its head and most of its body hid under the vegetation. She scanned the area, attempting to better assess the snake's exact location. Her heartbeat quickened.

A rattling sound emanated from somewhere in the foliage. It shook the air with urgency. A shaking sound that shortened her breath. *Was it venomous?* Next, the loudest hissing she ever heard came from this animal. It was like air rushing from a car tire. An area of plants quivered, and the shadowy form of the snake could be seen through the leaves. Its head rose up into plain view, and coiled back, looking at her with its dark eyes. A long forked tongue tasted the air, sensing her presence. Its head signaled warning coloration, with blood red scales covering its jaw and throat. The rest of it was a glossy obsidian, that glistened with a deep blue iridescence. Her gaze locked with the big black eyes of the snake. Still hissing, its mouth gaped open. Mara caught her breath, and thought she could see fangs. With neck coils fully taught, it unleashed and struck at her.

Mara screamed as she jumped back, with both feet leaving the ground. Cyndra's gift flew off into the bushes. Spinning around, she dove into her car, slammed the door, and sped off. Both her heart and lungs hammered her chest. After fumbling for the inhaler, she took a few deep breaths. Even with the AC on max, streams of sweat poured from her brow. Of all days, why did Emilio have to be out sick today? This was supposed to be *his* job. She took a drink, and fortunately was only a minute away from her house.

At home, she flung open the door to the psychotronic room. "I'm never setting foot in that God awful place again," said Mara, exasperated. "I barely escaped being bitten by a monster snake."

Griff, on the computer, kept his gaze on the screen as he answered, "Stay put then; our job here will be over before you know it." He managed to pull himself away from the monitor and asked, "Where did you leave the amplifier?"

"It's just outside Cyndra's house, where that vile creature attacked me."

"That's okay, it seems to be working better than expected. I'm picking up Cyndra in what appears to be their laboratory."

Mara sat down and had another drink. Her phone lit up with a text from the professor at Caloosa:

Florida grasshopper sparrow, endemic and endangered.

Her green eyes fluoresced with excitement as she pondered the implications. Daemon's toads devoured a rare, federally protected bird that lived only here in Florida. The toads weren't the only thing chowing down; social media would eat this up. She sent out a group text with this information to her friends still at the Elysium tour, giving them extra ammunition for the protest they had planned. A message to Jack Landon followed, informing him that El Dorado would officially make Elysium Jungle off limits to its residents. That vermin infested garden presented a hazard to both the public and the environment, and everyone should avoid contact with it. She also informed Jack to proceed with the code enforcement concerns with Elysium that had been on hold. Sending the 'toads eating birds' scenario to her information technology specialists, she requested the creation of some memes and to flood the internet with that message. Mara sat back in her chair and sipped her champagne. "Destroying someone's life can be challenging," she said, taking a deep breath, "but so satisfying."

Griff switched to another monitor and searched social media. Articles condemning Elysium along with the memes started to come in. A parade of images and videos of the toad gobbling up the helpless screeching baby birds, appeared with various captions:

Grasshopper Sparrow - Tasty, to the Marrow
A Despotic Exotic that Thrives on Demise
Taste Buds Singing & Ecological Alarms Ringing

"I love the lyrical quality," Mara said. "Dr. Lev's team is so talented."

"They're picking up lots of hits. It's going to go viral," he said, then shifted his attention back to the psychotronic device that was finally ready to monitor Cyndra. Mara looked on as Griff adjusted the settings.

He activated the quantum remote viewing feature of his equipment. This produced a real time video feed of the target, Cyndra, displayed on his large monitor. Various settings allowed the image to be adjusted; zooming in or out, or changing the angle of view. A column of text appeared along the right side of the image, describing her state of mind, even individual thoughts could be registered. A small icon of a moth appeared at the top of the screen. This enabled an artificial intelligence connection with the moths that had been programmed into the network. There were many other features, but this provided plenty to get started. As they became comfortable with its operation, the mind altering technology would soon be deployed, sending negative thoughts of Daemon into her mind. Mara and Griff watched as Cyndra appeared on the monitor, sitting in the lab, talking to Katashi.

In the lab, Katashi analyzed data from soil samples as Cyndra sat across the counter from him. She kept up to date with current events on her phone, which she snuck with her today. He looked up, "The abundance of magnetic bacteria is incredible. I've never seen such species density."

Cyndra nodded. "In this place, there's plenty of density to go around."

Katashi's eye brow raised for a moment, he then continued. "Last night at the fire ceremony, the way you moved was... phenomenal."

"With all that drumming and a few nectars, I was zoned."

His gaze toward Cyndra deepened. "I hope you don't mind my asking, but is there a thing between you and Daemon?"

Cyndra's lips pressed together, then spoke, "He's an intriguing guy, but sometimes I'm not so sure. He does some dumb things, like firing Emilio." She threw her arms in the air. "And he gets all conspiratorial on Mara. She's so wonderful and generous. I don't understand."

"Daemon's definitely got a different perspective on life," he said diplomatically. "In his own way he can be very giving."

"Sure, giving out hard work," she said, rubbing her lower back. "Sometimes I wish he would go deep into his jungle and never come out."

"Remember, he's under a lot of pressure right now. Emilio is gone, and Armando is out sick today, so each of us need to perform as best we can." He clicked print, the machine whirred, and rolled out some hard copies. After a brief inspection, he looked again at Cyndra. "I'm not trying to be a jerk, but Daemon should be back soon, and didn't he want you to fertilize the garden with ash from the fire?"

Cyndra recalled her previous experience of being covered with dirt from spreading rock powders. "Yep, the zombie dust again." Her fingers streaked across the phone as she scanned messages.

"Hey, that's an important job. Ash is loaded with monoatomic elements; it's considered sacred in some cultures."

"Okay, you're right. I guess it's the heat that's getting to me." She began to stare blankly at her phone.

Katashi scrolled down his screen and continued to decode secrets in the soil. He printed out more copies.

Cyndra's eyes fluttered, and her vision blurred. A sound hummed and buzzed inside her head. Her face flushed and she began to sweat. "I don't know what's going on, did the AC go off?" She wavered on her seat.

Katashi dashed around the counter and closed in on Cyndra. "What can I do to help?" he asked. "How about some ice water?"

"Yes," she said, her hand covered her heart as it began to race. The room began spinning. She took a sip of ice water, then splashed the rest into her face. The glass tilted, and its contents poured out. Ice cubes slid across the floor. Next, the glass slipped out of her hand, shattering on the tile.

Katashi grabbed his phone and called Daemon… just voicemail. He called the Sales Center, same result.

Cyndra gasped for air, and blurted out, "Daemon is a monster, he must be stopped!"

Katashi froze, startled at Cyndra. He probed into her puzzling outburst, "What's going on?"

She attempted to speak again, but her mouth just hung open a few moments before closing. Readjusting her seated position, and wiping excess water from her face, she began to get more centered. The dizziness ebbed as she strained to understand her outburst. Her hands trembled while rubbing her neck. Gazing downward, she whispered, "I don't know why I said that. Those words seemed to come from somewhere else."

Katashi moved closer and put his hand on her shoulder. "You've been dealing with a lot of stress lately, just relax, it'll be okay," he said reassuringly.

"Don't say anything to Daemon, he has enough to worry about," she whispered, and slowly helped herself up to standing. "I'm going outside for some fresh air."

"Be careful," Katashi said, as she hobbled out the door.

Members of the garden tour, fueled by disgust with the invasive toads, coalesced into a protesting crowd in the parking area. A local news van pulled up, and a reporter and cameraman climbed out. The cameraman was tall and heavy, clad in denim with his hair pulled back in a pony tail. The woman reporter was slender and energetic. The crowd chanted "Stop killer toads" and "Clean up the jungle."

Daemon followed the mob and attempted to calm

them down. Some of the more vocal activists drowned him out. As the cameraman approached, Daemon spoke up, "Elysium is doing what we can to address the problem of invasive animals in Florida." The crowd jeered. "Over the years, we have provided prime habitat for many native species." Angry voices disagreed all around him.

The reporter asked, "What is your purpose in breeding one of the most toxic, invasive animals on earth?"

"I'm not intentionally breeding them; they simply inhabit most of south Florida. Everyone needs to calm down." His pulse increased.

"There are reports that you feed them psychoactive plants to make them more aggressive and poisonous."

"That's ridiculous," he said, wagging his finger. "This is a research center using plants to improve brain function."

"Do you have any plans to exterminate this plague?" she said, maneuvering around so the cameraman could include more protesters in the background.

"It's not a plague, and over time ecological systems will make adjustments."

"In light of the public threat, are you going to follow the will of the people and close down?

"This is my own business; I'm not obligated to the whims of radical protesters. We're not closing. This is just mob hysteria." His brow furrowed.

"Such a blatant disregard for public safety, Mr. Makarios, do you consider yourself an elitist, above the law?"

"That's enough. This is private property; you need to leave now," he said, pointing in the direction of the parking lot exit.

"I understand. You want to cover this up, to hide what's really going on. But it's too late, Mr. Makarios, you and your criminal operation have now been exposed," she said, climbing back into her vehicle.

The van drove off and the crowd began to disburse. Daemon caught his breath, and headed back to the lab when his phone rang.

Mara spoke, "Hello, Daemon, just letting you know El Dorado Village is advising all residents to avoid your invasive species farm for the sake of their own health and safety. Also, there were some knit picky code enforcement issues we had previously neglected, but now they'll be coming at you full force. We want everything to be orderly, don't we? Thought I'd give you a little heads up."

"You, and your new world order friends will not be missed."

"I know you don't really mean that; are you aware of the old motto, 'Order from chaos'? Your disorderly environment naturally attracts people who want to tidy things up a bit. And how do you like the free publicity?" Mara said with a snarl.

"You set this all up, didn't you? How?"

"Oh, don't worry about all that behind the scenes stuff; what really matters is... problem-reaction-solution. Such a wonderful formula to manufacture a better world, don't you agree?"

"Why are you doing this Mara? What do you want?"

the phone heated up against his ear.

"You know what I want, my company already offered you well above market value for your garden, and you refused. Now you've forced us to take more drastic measures."

"Why do you want Elysium so badly. Is it vortex energy?"

"I believe I'll let that question spin naturally in your mind for a while," she said and snickered.

"Whatever you've got planned, it isn't going to work." Daemon's pace increased, as he approached the lab.

"Daemon, you're dreaming," she said, " and I suggest you dream of antidotes, because what's coming is your most poisonous nightmare."

Daemon stormed into the lab to find Katashi and Shavonda staring at the computer. He shook out tension from his body, and allowed himself to be more present.

"We have a situation going on," said Shavonda. "It's about the cane toads. You're on the local news, on social media, all over. For once, it's a good thing you don't like to go out in public."

Daemon hovered in front of the computer screen in disbelief. A relentless barrage of accusations, photos and videos condemning him and Elysium. "Do what you can to mitigate this. Hire a service to salvage our online reputation."

Shavonda turned to Katashi, "Get the most highly rated service you can find, we're going to need it."

"Let's do what we can for now to resolve this, but

139

don't let it become a big distraction. Remember, we have a fast approaching deadline."

They hired a company to quell the digital storm. Daemon responded to his personal email and phone messages. The mood settled.

Katashi mapped out energetic pathways between magnetic bacteria, mycorrhizal fungi, and plants that exhibited exceptional nootropic qualities. Shavonda processed recently harvested plants, and each day the chemical investigation grew more complex than the last. Daemon reviewed notes on all aspects of this research. In order to make a big discovery, he kept expanding his view.

Shavonda stepped into the dehydration room to gather more samples. Upon returning she exclaimed, "Those plants are getting so aromatic, you could practically get high hanging out in there."

"You would know all about that, wouldn't you," said Katashi, with a wink.

Daemon turned to Katashi, "Give me your most promising sample, and I'll give it a whirl," said Daemon.

Katashi handed over the liquid extract. "Bon apatite."

Downing the bitter sweet liquid, Daemon maneuvered himself into a comfortable position. "This feels good so far," he said, closing his eyes for a moment to tune in more deeply. Reopening his eyes, he could see with high definition. Even though the increased sensory acuity was great, he was more amazed at the feelings that warmed his heart. "Where is Cyndra?" he asked, realizing he hadn't seen her since early morning. He became deeply concerned about her welfare.

"She went to spread the ash, despite not feeling well," said Katashi. "I'll call her, maybe she's at home." He dialed and paused, "Hmm, no answer."

Daemon sat down and again closed his eyes to focus more deeply. Cyndra's refreshing, buoyant energy filled his heart and mind. Sensing her at the center of the garden, near the fire pit, he stood up abruptly. "Okay, keep processing the information, I'm going to check on her," he said, as he ran out the door.

Daemon didn't slow down until he approached the middle of his forest. He saw white and grey patches of powder strewn on the ground, evidence that Cyndra had been spreading the ash as instructed. Following the winding path to the fire pit, he spied her laid out on the ground in the shade. White ash completely covered her face, arms and legs. Daemon knelt beside her, looking for signs of life. *What could have happened?*

She opened her eyes and smiled.

Daemon gave a sigh of relief and returned the smile. "Are you feeling okay? You look very pale." His dark eyes gleamed.

"I'm actually starting to embrace this living dead look," she said. "It's so gothic." She sat up and explained. "I felt pretty bad earlier, but came down here anyway. Once I started throwing the ashes around, I began to feel better. I thought, if a little helped, then a lot would be great, so I covered myself in it. It worked. I felt insulated, protected, and restored. It was like this white powder deflected any darkness. I ended up laying down... guess I fell asleep."

"Glad you're okay, I was concerned." Grabbing her hands, he helped pull her up to standing. Observing her pallid state, he spoke, "Don't worry, you don't look like a zombie... more like a ghost."

"Very funny," she said as she playfully punched him in the arm. As she did, a plume of dust burst from all over her body.

"Where did you get such an explosive temper?" he asked with a smile.

"I don't think I had one until I met you."

"I know I can be difficult, but hopefully my work can evoke a sense of wonder."

"Your work does make me wonder."

They ambled back in silence. The soft path tunneled through a jade forest, resplendent with flowers, and kaleidoscopic butterflies flickered through shards of sunlight.

In the lab, Daemon finished up the day's work with Katashi and Shavonda, while Cyndra showered off at home with the rest of the day off. The final brain diagram print outs for the day slid through the printer. They included information on various vital signs such as respiration and heart rate. Katashi and Shavonda left, leaving Daemon at his computer checking Elysium's online sales. The bad publicity from the toads not only wiped out any sales for today, but some customers actually requested refunds from previous purchases. Advertisers pulled out. He stretched his neck, and took a deep breath. Checking his email, he opened up a message from Caloosa University.

Mr. Makarios,
It has come to the review board's attention that a recent inspection was made of your facility regarding the trial period of a work-study program. Unfortunately, the results from your evaluation did not meet our standards. The student, Cyndra Faye, was not only absent from her duties, her location was completely unknown. Living conditions were deplorable, and there was no record of her activities. In addition, there is concern about your proclivity toward invasive species. Regrettably, we are forced to suspend our relationship with your establishment at this time.

Daemon expected as much. No need to disturb Cyndra now with the news, it could wait until tomorrow. Not wanting to upset Lynette while visiting her sister, he also waited to notify her.

Sitting up tall, he remembered his goal. Trying to imagine the happiness and success that Utopia Nectar would bring to himself and many others proved difficult. He gazed out the window and pondered his fate. In the late afternoon sky, shimmery cumulus clouds condensed and darkened. Daemon shut off the computer. The counter full of extracts called to him. He mindfully combined a few, and gulped it down. Grabbing the brain scan printouts, he tacked them onto a wall; a montage of diverse states of brain activity.

He stared at the images as lightning flashed and etched the information into his consciousness. He practiced his beam of light meditation. Daemon channeled energy and information through his mind and body. The storm charged up his thoughts, and magnetically stirred feelings, especially for Cyndra. She appeared in his mind, as she was earlier, covered in white ash. As lightning struck, her image flashed to pure white light, that faded into an afterglow deep within his heart. He effervesced, as a soft, soothing radiance flowed through his whole body. Opening his eyes, he returned from his inner journey with new insight into the elusive formula. *Balance the electrical, thinking brain with the magnetic, feeling heart.*

As the storm passed, he restarted the computer and scanned the files for plants and fungi that had tested with a higher magnetic potential. He discovered correlations with herbs that affected the heart. Relationships and patterns between plants and various physiological processes lit up his mind. Thankfully, the program provided loads of information. Daemon worked tirelessly, late into the night.

Cyndra sat on the couch, savoring a slice of vanilla cake. Nisha sat in the living room window, blending in with the outside darkness. Looking into the garden, her ears tilted and turned following the movement of sounds. As Cyndra finished her snack, Mara called.

"Hello Cyndra, hope it's not too late."

"It's okay, I'm a night owl."

"I trust Daemon isn't working you too hard," Mara rasped.

"I'm fine," she said, gazing at her furry companion.

"Yes, indeed you are. Your father should be proud."

"I wouldn't know," she said shortly.

"Did your father work you to the bone like Daemon?"

"Not really." Feeling restless, she stood up from the couch and began walking around the room.

"Do you see Daemon as handsome?"

"Sure, he's okay."

"I believe he's interested in you, but perhaps it's an adoration, like a father for his daughter." Mara's voice grew more breathy.

"Let's talk about something else." Her voice strained as her pace quickened.

"I would be remiss if I didn't warn you about a monstrous serpent that dwells in the vicinity of your house."

"I saw the shed skin. Daemon said it's large but harmless." She glanced out the window.

"He'll say anything to distract from the truth. What is he actually doing about the toads? They're everywhere day and night."

"That's a good question."

"I'm concerned about you Cyndra, laboring in that sultry jungle, unclean and spent."

"It's really not too bad."

"No, Cyndra, it's dreadful. Currently, it's a steam bath outside. You can almost feel that wet heat penetrating your little adobe, can't you?"

"I guess so." She returned to sitting on the couch.

"Can't you imagine feeling feverish, moistened all over from excretions. You're panting and gasping for

145

release."

Cyndra's face flushed. "I suppose it does feel stuffy."

"Utilize the Jasmine and orange blossom oils I gave you. Apply them completely over your body; they're cool and refreshing."

"I've already blended some of them into a carrier oil, ready to apply."

"Excellent. Just get comfortable, lay down, and indulge yourself. Cyndra, it's late, I won't keep you. Sleep well, and extra sweet dreams tonight... sticky sweet."

Cyndra shed her clothes and applied the oils as she prepared for sleep. She yielded to the bed's soft support, and her mind grew more quiet. As her breathing slowed, her hands and feet tingled. It was similar to what was sometimes felt in the garden, however, it did not recede or stop, but continued and grew stronger. Waves of vibration rolled through her entire body. Tactile, yet almost audible, like a magnetic murmur. They elicited delicious feelings, like the over indulgence of a velvety dessert, along with its resulting lethargy. Lapped by sweet, whispering waves, she listed into sedation and sleep.

Simmering and seething waves engulfed her attention. Frothy and fizzy, the sound evolved into a hiss, becoming loud and invasive. It razzed and short circuited her nerves, leaving her incapacitated. Daemon entered her room as she laid motionless in bed. He carried the indigo snake, hissing as its polished black body draped and crawled over his shoulders. His dark eyes smoldered with passion as he edged toward her.

Standing close he said, "You belong to me," as he laid the snake down onto her body. The lanky reptile stretched out and elongated to many times its original length. It slid around and encircled her neck. Coils entwined her arms and tightened. Scaly loops encircled and pinned her legs, as its long body held down all parts of her. Daemon's hand slid behind her head as his face came close to hers. His breath brushed her cheeks and lips. She smelled cologne; it was a familiar scent, what her father wore. Daemon kissed her, and said, "You're my little princess." That haunting phrase tore through her mind and body. She squeezed her eyes shut, and tugged against the dark bondage. The coils compressed her throat. She struggled to breathe. The coils grew tighter, and everything turned black.

Cyndra awoke, stumbled to her bathroom, and vomited in the toilet.

"You like her, don't you?" Griff said as he opened the door to the psychotronic room.

Mara sat up; her eyes not quite focused. An empty champagne glass sat on a nearby table. The psychotronic device displayed a still shot of Cyndra lying naked in bed. She reached over and turned it off. It took a moment for her to catch her breath, "Don't be silly, I'm just observing her."

"Looks like you're having a really good time doing it," Griff said, leaning in closer to check the equipment.

"It doesn't hurt to enjoy your work now and then,"

she said, pouring another drink.

"What work? You've got the device set on sexual arousal. You're getting her excited. Looks like the feeling could be mutual."

"I was testing the parameters of this equipment. The directions state that if the operator causes a subject to have positive feelings such as euphoria, the settings can be adjusted to channel their life energy back to the operator. Some kind of quantum bio-feedback entanglement." She dabbed some moisture from her face and added, "It's fantastic, better than any drug."

"Keep this up and you're going to fry your nerves," his gaze shifted back and forth form her to the equipment. "Whatever happened to programming Cyndra to hate Daemon?"

"You can't run hate all the time, it'll destroy her. After all, I'm an artist. Stirring up different moods is like blending colors on a palette. It's a process, a creative journey of discovery."

"You're becoming obsessed with her."

"No more than you obsess about finances."

"The nationalists are giving us a hard time all over the globe. I'm doing everything I can to keep us afloat."

"Look, we've both got our own jobs to do. You manipulate the numbers, and I'll manipulate the minds."

Day Nine

"Knowledge becomes evil if the aim is not virtuous."
Plato

Mara awoke in her dimly lit bedroom gasping for air. She sat up and fumbled for her inhaler. Attempting long deep inhales in vain, she struggled against the relentless shortness of breath. The uncontrollable panting awakened Griff.

"Mara, that sounds bad," he said, jumping out of bed. "I'm calling an ambulance." He paced while talking to emergency personnel. Glancing out their bedroom window, he noticed something odd. Their lush green lawn glowed white in the early morning twilight. He turned to Mara, "They're on their way, I'll be back in a minute." He scrambled downstairs, and flung open the front door for a closer look. Mushrooms, thousands of white mushrooms encircled the whole house, extending out about 30 feet all around. Slamming the door, he huffed back up the stairs. "I think I know what's wrong. Our property's engulfed by mushrooms. You must be reacting to the spores." He helped her over to the window.

Hunched over and breathless, she stared down at the ghostly invasion. Her pallid complexion reflected the blue, predawn light. "That's Daemon's work," she garbled, "his time is up."

149

Mara sat up in her hospital bed, her vital signs stabilized. Griff sat next to her, managing business from his phone.

Scrolling through her photos of Daemon's garden, she spoke in a gravelly voice, "Get our Caloosa biologist to identify those mushrooms ASAP, and investigate Daemon's garden." She kept searching the images until one caught her eye. Enlarging the photo, it revealed perhaps the same mushrooms that invaded her property. "I thought I recalled seeing them." She cleared her throat. "And get a hold of our friend at the sheriff's department, make sure everything goes smoothly."

"I'm on it," said Griff.

Color returned to Mara's complexion as she felt more in control of the situation. "Get the landscaping company, have them remove the fungal invested lawn, and lay down new sod. I want it done now, before we return home later today."

"Consider it done," said Griff.

A nurse entered the room, checking Mara's condition. "Glad to see you're doing okay now." She pressed a few buttons on a monitor. "You had our immunologists perplexed for a while; that allergen you contracted was very strange." She turned and continued her rounds.

Elysium Jungle effervesced in the strong morning sun. Volatile oils and nervine laced flower nectars inspired the air, evaporating toward the heavens like a botanical prayer. Chirps and warbles echoed through the trees. An occasional cane toad plopped into view, looking over its new menu of diurnal fauna.

Despite the urgency of the nectar research, Daemon's team needed a little break, and worked from home today. Daemon began this morning by meeting with Azarias. They savored a soothing cup of holy basil tea while inhabiting the lanai. Their conversation mirrored not only the light filled forest around them, but also its shadows.

"Today I'm leaving to comfort an ailing family member in Tarpon Springs," said Azarias, and sipped some tea. "This will be our last meeting for some time."

Daemon sighed and said, "I understand…I appreciate the time you've already given me. You've deepened my connection to nature and myself."

"Say more about that," said Azarias.

"The pillar of light meditation has made me more aware of lightning. I feel it coming, I'm more present and inspired."

"Anything else about nature?"

"I'm more aware of the communication of bees through different tones of buzzing. Their sense of direction and energetic purpose encourage me to pursue my goals, no matter what."

"Good, but also remember that your inner world is ultimately more important than the outer world."

A flock of white ibis wafted into an acacia tree near the lanai. Their snowy plumage stood out against the deep verdant leaves. Azarias turned and watched the graceful birds. "You're working with positive, light filled energy, but have you noticed any negativity, darkness?"

Daemon cradled his chin in his hand, "Hmm, to some extent, but for the most part I just feel more empowered each day, despite external events."

"Usually, there is balance between increased positive energy and the release of negative patterns." Azarias slid his hand through his silver hair. "But....everyone is different. How has Mara been acting lately?"

"She's generated a lot of bad press, but it's not going to kill me."

"Good." Azarias leaned toward Daemon. "In your heightened state of being, honoring all kingdoms of life, Utopia is already present. Trust that you will manifest it in a form the rest of humanity can realize."

Chills ran through Daemon. "Thanks for your reassurance."

Azarias explained that Daemon's rapid progression with his metaphysical work could create a corresponding backlash of dark energy. The greater the light, the greater the shadow that it cast. Azarias looked deeply into Daemon's eyes. "To win this conflict, utilize your connection with nature to its fullest, and dive deep into the essence of who you are."

Feeling empowered from his mentor's visit, Daemon called Lynette, although it was a bad connection. "Do you have a definite return date?"

"I'll be there four days from now. Is everything alright? I saw an article about you and venomous toads. What's going on? Is Cyndra okay?"

"Cyndra's fine, everything is okay. A few crazy environmentalists, but nothing to worry about," Daemon said, in a rather convincing tone. "There is, however, one thing you could do. I've heard rumors of some unscrupulous practices concerning Psi-Matics Global. Maybe you could look into that."

"Okay, I'll see what I can uncover."

Daemon tasted a new extract as his mind played out scenarios between Mara's illegal activity, the possible nullification of contracts, and how everything might shake out. His phone rang, it was Mara. The mere direction of his thoughts seemed to invoke her presence.

"I'm not sure how you conjured up those mushrooms around my house, but it's going to take more than some disgusting fungus to stop me."

"What mushrooms? You sound more delusional than ever."

"The same species you're growing throughout your garden. Let's see, I've got the name right here…blue meanies, *Panaeolus cyanescens*. Does that ring a bell?"

Daemon cringed. She got him. He did not like growing anything illegal, but he wanted to introduce psychedelic chemistry into the garden, not just through plants but also fungi. Although he grew fly agaric, a legal, yet mild psychedelic mushroom, he desired something with more potent chemistry. Ounce per ounce, blue meanies produced fantastic results. Despite their strong effects, few people, other than enthusiasts knew of them.

Mara continued, bringing Daemon back to the present. "Are you still there? The point is there's a sheriff on the way to close you down because of those mushrooms."

"They grow in tropical areas all over the world," he said in his defense. "Just like the cane toads, they're now a part of our environment."

"You can make your case in court. And don't forget your other upcoming cases, like the needless suffering of Brad Johnson. We'll all breathe easier once the FDA shuts down your production of those nasty nectars."

"Mara, you can't do this," he said, with a locked grip on his cell phone, while bolting from room to room.

"Enjoy your down time, Daemon, you'll need it."

Daemon's heart pounded. He opened a cabinet and took some Morpheus Nectar to calm down, then collapsed on the couch. He breathed deeply, and looked inward like Azarias recommended. Observing his fear, all of its connections throughout his mind became more clear. The triggers, the buzz words, the events that most frightened him were transformed into pure information. Without the emotional attachment, these mental patterns could more easily be reconstructed into a positive perspective. He quietly realigned his thoughts until abruptly shaken by a loud knocking at the door.

A hefty sheriff stood at the entrance and asked, "Sir, I am looking for the owner of this establishment, a Mr. Daemon Makarios."

"You found him," Daemon said.

The officer pronounced Daemon's property officially closed while an investigation ensued. "You are allowed to stay here if you choose, but no in or out traffic. Mr. Makarios, are any other individuals here on premises?"

"No, it's just me." He didn't want to interrupt Cyndra's stay.

"Very good. Anyone else would be required to leave at this time."

"Just do what you need to do."

"FYI, myself and other officers will take turns guarding the entrance." The sheriff stepped outside, wedged himself into his squad car, and drove back to the entrance of the driveway. In the distance, Daemon watched as he ran police tape across the private entrance, then planted himself firmly in his car.

Daemon went to the guest house to give Cyndra the news. Not only was she out of the work study program, but also now on lockdown; stuck here with only Daemon. Without much money between them, and Cyndra not having a car, it was not practical to send her to a hotel. They both decided she would stay. Her aunt would be back in a few days, and this ridiculous lockdown should be over before then. It seemed reasonable. He returned to the lab to finish his research for the day.

The sky darkened to grey and black. Leaves dashed through the air, and window screens moaned. The air cooled and freshened. Daemon felt the lightning on its way, and turned off the lab. Taking an extract, he looked out the window, and enjoyed the storm. He sensed waves of electromagnetic energy rolling through the garden as the day came to a close.

Cyndra sat on the couch with Nisha. "Don't worry, it's all going to be okay," she said, as she patted her furry head.

Nisha rubbed her face against Cyndra's hand.

"Daemon seems to want to help us," she continued, "but why do I have a sneaky suspicion he is working against us?"

Nisha nibbled her hand.

"Hey, no biting," she said, jerking her hand away.

Nisha crouched down and her ears flattened.

A brilliant flash and a deafening boom caused Cyndra to jump and Nisha to vanish under the couch.

"Whew," she said as her hand went to her heart, "the lightning here is insane." Forgetting about Daemon, she huddled up with a romance novel, taking herself into another world. After enjoying the temporary escape through several chapters, she set the book down. The storm had passed, and Nisha slept curled up next to her. She called her friend Tammy in Indiana, and brought her up to date with her challenging situation. Their conversation turned to snap chat. The weird and whimsical looks carried her away again on a vacation from her turmoil. After the call, she guzzled some Morpheus Nectar, attempting to use dreams as a distraction.

Cyndra, bathed in diffuse light, gazed out her bedroom window at the moon, growing closer to being full. She completely undressed, allowing her opalescent skin to harmonize with the ethereal ambiance. She communed with her feminine nature, imbued with charm and allure, yet entangled with foreboding. She lowered herself onto her bed, where she sat and attempted to resolve or at least accept this inner conflict. After some fruitless deliberation, she arrived at a temporary truce, that she simply needed some sleep. Her sleek frame stretched and lengthened between the smooth sheets. Gazing at the shadowy ceiling, she inhaled cool and refreshing aliveness. She exhaled any staleness and tension. As her breathing relaxed and became more quiet, the sounds of the night amplified and echoed inside her. The elevated trill of insects, and the bombarding percussion of cane toads, attuned her more deeply to the night realm.

A familiar tapping at her bedroom window evoked a smile. Tap, tap, tap, occult sphinx moths bumped against the glass. Her twilight friends desired her company. The silky purr of their wings softened her face. Their velvety sound buffered out any unwanted noise. She closed her eyes. Her soft form opened up to luxurious comfort and support, as she unfurled into sleep like an exquisite night blooming flower. Anointed with oil of jasmine, she intermingled with the seductive quality of the night, where pheromones, fragrant nectars, and multifarious dark essences conjured up dreams and desires.

The moths fluttered more strongly, and the tone became more forceful. It grew louder and louder, reminiscent of the deep hum of a power station. As the sound filled the room, she realized it was now originating from inside her room. Another presence occupied her space. A giant moth, about the size of her own body, hovered directly over her. What seemed

157

comforting a few moments ago, had grown into something ominous. Its wings were a blur as they beat fast and hard to support its large, robust, tubular body. The air churned like several ceiling fans on high. The rapid pulse generated not only air flow, but also a magnetic field with levitational effects. Cyndra's hair was floating and waving, although her body remained motionless in sleep paralysis. Objects on her night stand floated off, then fell to the floor. The bed sheet rippled. Some areas wafted and lifted, revealing her legs. The willful and powerful magnetic breeze persisted, levitating the entire sheet off of Cyndra's body, and flung it on the floor next to the bed. Any barrier between her and the moth was swept away, as this enigmatic creature exposed not only her body, but even unveiled hidden areas of her mind.

The moth uncoiled its proboscis. This long, slender, feeding tube reeled down onto Cyndra's face, as if dipping into a nectar rich blossom. The lively cable glided across her hairline, and slithered around her eyes. It lingered around her lips before sliding into her mouth. The snake-like probe explored her tongue and teeth. From the back of her mouth, it slid upward and emerged into her brain. Her face paled. Her eyes faded to an icy blue. The moth fed on Cyndra's consciousness. Her brain activity dulled, yet it spawned relief from her anxious, overactive mind.

Next, the moth's smooth rope-like appendage slid down her throat and snaked itself inside her chest. It bled her heart of sadness and pain, but drained away inspiration and hope.

The moth's sleek member descended into her gut. It sucked up lower frequency emotions like greed and fear. She felt lighter, yet disconnected.

The moth exploited Cyndra more deeply, as its smooth organ quivered inside her pelvis. It vibrated with a demanding desire to acquire her succulent ambrosia. She shook to the bone, as it unleashed a dark part of her, a compulsive need for desecration. Disturbed passion discharged through her viscera. It echoed childhood patterns of abuse; however, the overflowing of sensuous waves masked the pain, and drowned out any resistance. Lavish tingles flowed through every fiber of her being, melting her into sublime submission. Her breathing labored, her heart pounded, and she seized up. Her legs pulsed apart, unveiling a portal of desire. She gasped as the moth's tongue throbbed into her most sensitive spots, exactly what her body craved. She held her breath as the flood gates released an infra-red tsunami of sensation. Pounded with shock waves of searing nirvana, her body thrashed up and down on the bed. She screamed and spasmed with ecstasy. Every cell flushed with blissful energy.

The moth's large spots glowed like full moons. Its wings blared, and within that repetitive beat pulsed a disembodied voice. A feminine voice that reverberated all around her. Cyndra pieced together the slivered words. The staccato vocals evoked a sense of familiarity. It was Mara, shouting 'Cyndra…you're mine…Cyndra,' which became more choppy until the voice degenerated into static. The moth's whole body grew more energetic and bright. The entire room seethed with heightened color, sound, and sensation. As its frequency increased, the moth shifted dimensionally, it effervesced into pure light and dematerialized. The room's energy settled down. Cyndra unwound with an unfathomable satisfaction unlike anything she had experienced. Internal quiet and stillness reined. There was a sense of completeness, then everything faded and disappeared.

Cyndra opened her eyes. She was awake. Although physically exhausted, her mind was unthinkably placid. She contemplated what just happened; a dream that felt more real than anything in her life. As she pushed herself up to a seated position, Nisha peeked from behind the dresser. Cyndra's hair fluffed in all directions, dewy skin covered her achy body, and she resonated with the subtle hum of contentment. Her phone and bed sheet were strewn on the floor, as she stared vacantly, and laid her head in her hands. *Was it just a dream? What's really happening?*

Mara's glazed emerald eyes came into focus. Her heart still raced as she pulled herself to a more upright position in the operator's chair. Anticipating Griff would soon be checking on her, she brushed her hair back into place, and dabbed her flushed face with a handkerchief.

"Mara, what's going on? I thought I heard you yelling," said Griff, stepping into the psychotronic room.

"I was just giving Cyndra some live auditory cues," she said, straightening out her clothing. "Tracking her responses to varying volumes and tones." On the table sat not only an empty champagne glass but an empty bottle as well.

"It looks like all you are tracking is her physical body," said Griff, crossing his arms.

"I know what it looks like, but I'm getting deep inside her head. I can almost anticipate her next move, her next thought." She helped herself up to standing.

"Remember how Dr. Lev warned us about getting emotionally involved with our targets. Weird things can happen, especially with advanced technology. You used to follow his directions explicitly." He uncrossed his arms with palms turned up. "What's happened?"

"Although Lev is brilliant and inspiring, we ultimately need to bend the rules depending on our circumstances. I know what I'm doing."

"Whatever," he said, pushing his hands into his pockets. "Aside from all that, I'm flying to London tomorrow, some critical business just came up. Will be back in a few days."

"Oh, okay. Hope things go well for you…for us." Mara understood the importance of their financial affairs, and was always willing to support Griff in that regard.

"While I'm gone, remember, don't get emotionally involved. Instead of enjoying your juicy bio-feedback, you could get slammed with bio-blowback."

Day Ten

"Ignorance is the root and stem of all evil."
Plato

The sun materialized a new day. Light flourished through Daemon's home office window, bringing much needed positive energy into his world. He sent dozens of emails in an attempt to reopen Elysium. Tired of the bureaucratic maze, he checked in on the status of the cane toad opposition. They declared not only destruction to toads but also to Daemon himself. Grimacing, he turned it off, and trekked over to the guest house to check on Cyndra.

Daemon and Cyndra sat at her kitchen table. "Do you need anything?" he asked.

Cyndra squirmed, "Just some little things…like *freedom*," she said with some snark.

Daemon winced. "We need to make the best of it. Would you like to help in the lab?"

"Nope, going to finish the novel, then hang out with my friends online." She sat up perky and defiant.

"Okay, I'll be around if you need me," he said as he left to do more enquiry.

Daemon stared at the image of a brain on his wide screen monitor. The computer color coded the various mental functions. Like a neuro-artist, he created both the appearance and formula for higher consciousness.

Creating a recipe, he chugged it down before going out to harvest more plants. On the way, he stopped by to see Cyndra once again.

"Maybe you'd like to get a few mangos, they're super sweet and creamy," he said, trying to encourage her.

"Well, okay, just for the mangos," she said, "I'm running low on desserts."

They followed the path, under a lush canopy, toward the center of the garden. The strong mid-day sun pierced through openings amid the layers of foliage. Patches of leaves glared in hot spots, while shadow obscured others. The air was thick and languid. Scarlet honeysuckle spiraled up tree trunks, where shimmering hummingbirds darted and hovered.

"I know I've been unlikable at times. I'm sorry things ended up this way. Is there anything I can do?" he asked.

"Forget about it, Daemon. It's too late," she said. Walking through the splintered light, highlights and shadows rolled over her taught, well defined form.

Daemon's head nodded. "Trust me, I get it; however, I wanted you to know you're the most special woman I've ever met."

"Is that supposed to impress me? Seems like I'm the *only* woman you've met, at least in a very long time." Her head tilted up.

"No, no, the point is, you're amazing. Smart, funny, capable, and beautiful." His magnetic eyes embraced her body and mind.

"Look, even though we had some moments, as of now, I'm definitely not interested. Just the way it is."

"Okay, whatever you want," he said, pointing and turning, "the mangos are this way."

Daemon pressed his fingers into the smooth, red and green skin to determine ripeness. He severed a couple of mangos from the tree with his clippers, and dropped them into his harvesting sack. "I've got some other collecting to do. I'll bring these over on my way back."

"Thanks," said Cyndra, as she turned and sauntered back to her oasis of cool air and internet access.

Daemon watched her departure, still not sure what bothered her so much. He turned and proceeded toward the center of the garden, as if a journey to the center of his mind. The collection of botanicals was like taking a personal inventory of his thoughts, expectations, and budding capabilities. Feeling complete with his harvest, he headed back. Cyndra accepted the mangos with few words. Returning to the lab to process the herbs, he buried himself in further exploration.

Cyndra laid on her couch, on the phone with Tammy, when a knock at the door interrupted her conversation. "I'll call you back later," she said, and opened the door, expecting Daemon.

"Hi Cyndra, good to see you again," said Emilio, slightly out of breath, and carrying a bag.

"I can't believe it," she said, smiling, "so good to see you. How did you get through the lockdown?"

"Climbed over the wall. No big deal, done it before," he said, in his usual nonchalant way.

"Have you been doing okay since Daemon let you go?"

"Sure, been working for Mara. That's why I'm here; this is from her." He reached in the bag, and pulled out a small box, gift wrapped in glossy red and black paper topped with a bow.

Cyndra held it and read an attached card.

Take this tonight, and everything will be revealed.
Mara

"Cyndra, take care of yourself. Got to go before Daemon or the sheriff see me." He dashed off into the garden, toward El Dorado.

Cyndra sat on the couch and began peeling away the smooth paper revealing a plain cardboard box. Opening it, she pulled out a bottle. It had a purple label, printed with the words Utopia Nectar. *Mara was right.* She told the truth about Daemon, that he had already created Utopia Nectar. She felt justified in her anger towards him. Apparently, the real goal of his research was finding financial gain.

"Tonight, I'm going to possess transcendent intelligence, become a goddess, a moon goddess," she said to her sable coated friend, sitting on the floor in front of her. It was late afternoon, and she wanted everything taken care of before her inner excursion. She poured plenty of crunchies into Nisha's food bowl. To fill the water bowl, she looked in the frig for bottled water, but she found only fruit juices and teas. Glancing around for some stray bottle, she noticed the clouds darkening, and asked Nisha, "Instead of bottled water, how about manna from heaven?" She set the empty bowl outside to be filled with rain water.

Rain and lightning poured down. Nisha hid under the couch and meowed. Cyndra snacked on some energy bars, waiting for the storm to finish. Afterwards in the shower, she washed away any resistance to transformation.

Although alone, she desired to look presentable for her divine experience. She slid into a satiny magenta dress, and applied matching mascara and lipstick. Gazing in the mirror, she appeared both sleek and otherworldly.

The sun journeyed behind the trees. Golden light fractured through the silhouetted forest. A cacophony of bird calls signaled the transitioning of worlds, from diurnal to nocturnal. This celestial voyage shifted frequency; amber rays scaled down to burnt orange. Under the advancing shadows, moon flowers spiraled open, releasing their heady scent. Massive cumulus clouds caught the last fragments of daylight, diffusing fuchsia and lilac through their vaporous, sculptured forms. The air grew more aromatic and heavy. Clouds darkened as the crossing over period continued. The heavenly glow dimmed and vanished, replaced by sparkles of sound from katydids and crickets. Cane toads joined the ensemble with their strobe-like drumming. As the voyage into night progressed, sooty clouds flashed erratically with heat lightning.

Sitting upright with anticipation, Cyndra lit some candles and invoked illumination. She desired to be more aware of her innate worthiness and power, and to be able to understand others and their true motives. After so many perplexing events and speculation, the question still arose, *do I really love Daemon or do I hate him?* She closed her eyes and prayed for resolution. Her complexion glowed with the soft tones of candle light. She felt a warmth in her heart as she determined to live a life that included a caring, loving relationship, at least with herself, whether or not that would include someone else. She released a deep sigh, and opened her eyes. Nisha jumped up on the couch next to her, as if adding support for her journey.

Cyndra peered into her box of essential oils. Each of them embodied and channeled a particular current in the river of life. For her spiritual makeover this evening, she chose oils that nourished her divine feminine nature. Picking up orange blossom, an uplifting floral with herbaceous notes, she anointed her forehead, with the intention of elevating her thoughts. With jasmine, a more sweet, evocative oil, she caressed her throat, requesting clear self-expression. She reached toward the center of her chest with rose, a complex and powerful scent, the essence of the spiritual heart; asking to be open to love. Ylang ylang, stroked onto her legs, increased her sensuality. She imagined dancing and moving like a goddess. The synergistic effect of all of these precious oils created an exalted allure, a supreme seductiveness, the kind that took a man's breath away. She stretched for a moment, swished her hair back, and sat with majestic stature. Her eyes reflected candle flames as she gazed upon her heavenly gift.

Lit up like an altar, the coffee table displayed the

bottle of Utopia Nectar. An iced glass of sugary coconut juice acted as a mixing agent, to mask the unpleasant taste as Mara had advised. A glass of ice tea served as additional refreshment. She opened the bottle of liquid paradise, and held it to her nose. Her face tightened as the scent alone made her gag. Unlike other nectars, the directions stated the dosage as being half a bottle, or ten droppers full. A much greater amount than the others, but it was after all, designed to produce a more incredible effect. She squirted the brown serum into the sweet, opalescent juice, and stirred with a spoon. She took a deep breath, a few quick gulps, and the sacrament was done. Her eyes squeezed shut and her mouth contracted. Afterwards, she rinsed down its residual taste with tea. Sitting back into the couch and gazing out the window, she spied the moon.

The moon, almost full, buoyed up over the charcoal outline of trees with a wild orange mood. Amphibian and invertebrate sounds merged into a multi phylum chorus. Tropical cactus buds opened, exposing their milky interiors, and releasing a sublime but musky scent, stirring animalistic desire. Silent heat lightning streaked low in the sky, level with the moon. The acrobatic maneuverings of bats mirrored the zig zag pathways of arcing electricity. As the moon rose higher, its color brightened to a Sulphur yellow. A screech owl shrieked and wailed with high pitched vibrato.

For Cyndra, the moon was easy on the eyes. Diffusing a soulful and sometimes melancholy nature, it spoke to her in a way that was difficult to describe, like a subconscious frequency. As its hypnotic attraction increased, her body tingled, yet her mind settled down. Her mouth became dry as paper, and she needed another drink. Wobbling up to standing, she was surprised by her lack of balance.

She wavered to the kitchen to get some fruit juice. On the way back she caught her reflection in the mirror, and stopped immediately. Her pupils dilated completely, making her eyes jet black. Alarmed at first, she then surmised it must be from the nectar. Strange and compelling, as if the windows of her soul opened up to an unfathomable darkness. Inexplicably charmed, she lingered with her new mysterious countenance. Eventually, this eerie look became self-intimidating, and she turned away. Faltering across the room, she tilted precariously toward the moon, as if pulled by a magnetic lure. Shifting her weight, she heaved herself back, and floundered onto the couch. Sitting up, she brushed back her hair, and assessed her situation. *Not feeling very different so far*. Removing the bottle cap, she gulped some juice, waiting for the nirvana to kick in.

Nisha meowed long and hard, sitting next to Cyndra on the couch. "What's wrong?" she asked and petted her head. Nisha meowed louder, then bit her hand. "Ouch, what has gotten into you?" Jerking her hand away, she shook out the stinginess. The meow deepened and turned into a growl. She flattened her ears and swished her tail. Almost like a Halloween cat, she arose onto all fours; the hair on her back stood up and her tail bushed out. Cyndra reached out, attempting to calm her furry friend. Instead, Nisha swatted at her, hissed, jumped down and sped into the bedroom.

Cyndra regrouped. She took a deep breath and sipped more juice. *This journey to the divine sovereign was turning out to be a royal pain.* Leaning back, she invited her muscles to unwind. Moonbeams cast through the window grew noticeably brighter.

A knock at the door jolted away her stillness. *It must be Daemon.* She staggered to the door and opened it. No one was there. Curious, she stepped outside, leaving the door open as she looked in every direction. She gasped at the landscape. Almost like daylight, an unbelievably powerful lunar radiance revealed an enchanted world. Foliage gleamed silver green, with jewel like beads of water from the earlier rain. Flowers luminesced in this inspiring light.

Finding some steadiness, she stood still and called out, "Hello, anybody there?" No response other than the ubiquitous chant of the night garden. Continuing to listen, a familiar sound emerged from the pervasive din. Fleecy wings vibrated and ruffled. Her nighttime companions, the occult sphinx moths, zoomed in close and hovered. Their long, thread like tongues tickled her face and neck, siphoning dewy sweetness. She smiled and communed with her night angels. Their murmuring flutter strummed her heart strings. "I love you guys," she said, and in doing so, noticed her mouth, once again parched. Driven by thirst, she returned inside and closed the door.

Cyndra gathered up drinks from the kitchen, set them on the coffee table, then settled again into the couch. Comfortably supported, she softened and sighed. Closing her eyes, she attempted to tune in more carefully to the elusive divine energy that must be on its way.

"Good evening, Cyndra," said Daemon.

Her eyes popped open as her head spun in the direction of his voice. "Oh my God, I didn't hear you come in," she said, pulling her hair back in place. As she stared at Daemon, her face paled, increasing the contrast with her dark eyes. She crafted a sense of composure and said, "Please sit down," patting the cushion beside her.

Daemon sat close to her, and placed his hand on her shoulder. "I see you've taken the Utopia Nectar." His eyes narrowed, and leaning in, his hand squeezed tight. "Be careful, it's not what you think it is." He spoke in deep and serious tones.

Cyndra raised her eyebrows, and her fingers fumbled with each other. "But Mara said it's fantastic."

Daemon glared. "Mara pretends to know things; she imagines she's one of the illuminated." His hand slid down to hers. "Beware, tonight you will face your shadow."

Cyndra's shoulders lifted and her face crinkled. "What does that mean?" Candle flames flashed across her eyes as her gaze shifted side to side.

His hand clasped around hers. "It's an unseen world that's all around you, that can become visible and dangerous. Evil is a reality." His gaze grew more stern as his lips pressed together.

Her head tilted to the side as she spoke, "I don't believe in evil as its own independent force. How do you know evil is real?" She leaned in for the answer.

"Evil is affecting us right now. It's powerful and real, even more real than me," he said flatly, his gaze remaining steady.

"What is that supposed to mean?" She looked deeply at him, her eyes, like black holes, sucking up all information around them.

"It means… I'm not actually real." He retracted his hand from hers, became still, and stared into her eyes.

Cyndra paused for a moment, then a big smile stretched across her face. "You're such a hoot," she said as she slapped his thigh and began to chuckle. "You had me for a second." She giggled and curled up with laughter. Her body heaved with a deep belly laugh; a welcomed release. She sat up refreshed, and turned toward Daemon, but only to find … he was gone. He had completely disappeared. She paused her breath, and craned her neck as she inspected the area. "Daemon, what's going on? This isn't funny anymore." She stretched across to the end of the couch and searched farther. Nothing. She collapsed down and buried her face in the cushions. *What's going on? This isn't Utopia. I don't know what to do.* Unable to think clearly, she laid still. As her body relaxed, her confusion also settled down. Eventually, she pulled herself up to sitting, and regrouped.

Candlelight cast dreadful shadows all around her. Outside, the beastly racket became more pervasive. The tumultuous night life called to her. Tuning in to the clamor, she sensed meaning within the croaks and peeps. A message embedded itself within nature's sounds. The various tones resolved into words, and sifting them together, she discerned the transmission. *"Welcome to the end of the world."* Once the words were deciphered, she couldn't help but hear them over and over as the night mantra droned on. She cupped her hands over her ears and bowed her head. The muffled messages turned back to harmless animal calls. Bent over, she released her hands down to her lap. She took a deep breath, then noticed a scent that unlocked caged memories. Woody and spicy, she smelled her father, and bolted upright.

"It's been a long time, Cyndra," said her father.

Her mouth hung open. Her black eyes like tar pits, graveyards of trapped lives. "It can't be you. How could you be here?" she exclaimed, shaking her head.

"How's my little princess doing?" he asked, in a casual manner, seemingly oblivious to her ruffled appearance.

"I hate you," she said, with venom. Her arms wrapped around her legs and folded them up close to her body.

"I couldn't help myself; it was you who seduced me." His hand reached toward her hair. "You're so beautiful."

She swatted his hand away. "Don't touch me."

"You're my blood; you'll always be mine."

"You don't own me." Her muscles tightened. "And one day, you'll get what you deserve."

"What I deserve is one more time with you." His lips crawled with lust.

"Get away from me, you're sick," she yelled, and shot up to standing, assisted by a flood of adrenaline. Although unstable, she swung her fist. Losing her balance, she fell and slammed onto the tile floor. The crash jolted throughout her body. Her knees throbbed and her wrists hurt. She pulled herself together and looked up. Unbelievably, her father was gone. Vanished.

Could he blend into the shadows that veiled the room? Into a disgusting substratum of existence? Is the obscurity of shadow just the unwillingness to see what is there? Overloaded, she began to shake. Dizzy with questions and regurgitated memories, she grew nauseous, crept to the bathroom, and got sick.

She flushed the toilet, and as it refilled, something moved inside. Underwater, a dark elongated form twisted and turned. The head of a large black snake broke the water's surface. Its red jaws agape as it undulated its tongue. She remained totally fixated on the creature while taking a slow step back. It's sleek body slithered up, and began pouring itself out and over the rim.

"Get away from me," she yelled. Aghast, Cyndra slammed the lid down onto its cold, scaly body. A quick hiss and the snake's head reached up, struck her forearm and held on tight. She shrieked as its curved teeth sank into her flesh. Blood trickled down her arm. The snake was substantial, so Cyndra positioned herself completely on the toilet lid, and pressed down with all of her weight. She bounced up and down, mashing its body. A deep crunch occurred as the snake's spine broke. It spasmed, released its grip, and the lifeless head of the snake dangled toward the floor. She lifted the lid and flushed again; the watery vortex sucked the snake down and away. Carefully rinsing off the grisly laceration, she assessed the damage, and wrapped it with a small cloth. Exhausted, she sunk down and sat on the bathroom floor. She closed her eyes and took time to rest and assimilate her experiences. *This can't be real. Nothing makes sense.*

Cyndra's eyes eventually opened, yet unsure if awake or dreaming. She stretched her achy body, and a cloth unraveled on her wrist. She removed it, and her wrist looked fine. *Why was it wrapped up to begin with?* She couldn't remember. Easing up slowly to prevent dizziness, she stood light as air, light as space. Walking through the house, she floated and drifted as if in a pool of water, but with no resistance. She saw Nisha's bowl of food. *Nisha... where is Nisha?* She searched throughout the house, calling her but getting no response. She looked under the bed and on top of the refrigerator. If she's not inside, she must be outside, although she never let her out.

Cyndra stepped outside. The moon, high in the sky, fully unleashed its magnetic energy to the plants, filling them with an ethereal vitality. An energy more subtle than the sun's vigor, but more magical. She searched for her lost friend. "Nisha, come here pretty kitty," she said as she explored. She spotted the forgotten water bowl, left out to fill with rain. Something occupied it. Looking closer, she gasped; a cane toad was soaking in it, poisoning the water. "Get out of there," she yelled as she kicked the bowl over along with the toad, both disappearing into the foliage. She remembered Daemon's warning. *But did he actually warn against it or just state what could happen, almost like giving a subliminal suggestion to actually create it?*

She investigated in every direction. Not far from her walkway, behind a small bush, she discovered Nisha, sprawled on the ground. She didn't respond to her name. Cyndra moved closer, "Nisha?" She reached down, placing her hand on its body. There was no warmth. Sliding her hands under the cat's body, she gently lifted her up. Her black satiny frame hung limp in her arms. No movement of her head, legs, or anything. "No, Nisha, you can't be…" She caressed Nisha's eyelids open to inspect her eyes. Just a blank stare. There was no sign of respiration. No sign of life at all. Nisha had been with her for so many years. Cyndra's only true friend here, now lost to this twisted menagerie, poisoned by those ugly creatures.

"I'm so sorry, Nisha. I've always loved you." She cradled her and hugged her tight. "I tried my best to protect you. All I wanted was for you to have a good life." Tears streamed down Cyndra's face. She held Nisha's soft body close for the last time, and whispered prayers to her spirit. Her sore knees wobbled as she found a space in the garden to lay her down. Cyndra picked fragrant flowers and limbs with lush foliage, and laid them down over the body. She amassed a beautiful, natural memorial for her special friend. With a final goodbye, and a vow to avenge her death, she left Nisha's body to the night.

Cyndra washed her hands in the bathroom sink. Viewing herself in the mirror, her eyes continued to elicit fascination. The big black orbs appeared curious and spooky, contrasted with her ghostly complexion.

Peeling away from her own mesmerizing look, she moved to the kitchen for another ice tea. Although light as air, paradoxically she felt tired, and shambled off to the bedroom. Shedding her clothes, she dropped into bed.

Lunar light blanketed Cyndra's pallid frame. Like a transdermal drug, it infused her skin with lucent analgesics. Subdued in a flood of celestial anesthesia, her vital signs slowed and became more spacious. This luminous opiate filtered into her mind, and she became more languid and quiet.

The moon traveled behind a thick bank of clouds. The bed room darkened. Cyndra's palliative light waned into obscurity. At first foreboding, she eventually found a sense of safety by becoming invisible in the darkness. Letting go of her old way of being, she released herself completely into shadow. In this dark world, she discovered unknown power.

TARGET OUT OF PHASE, RESET PARAMETERS / INSTALL NEW LINK

Mara researched the reason for this control panel display. With Griff in London, there would be no interruptions to her sessions monitoring Cyndra. How ironic that the psychotronic device failed to work now. She cursed the not so user friendly technical instructions, but eventually discovered the problem. Once Cyndra had consumed her gift, the angel's trumpet extract profoundly changed her electromagnetic signal to the extent that she no longer registered with the psychotronic device. Because Mara had developed such a strong mental and emotional link to Cyndra through this technology, if she changed her consciousness to somehow match Cyndra, the machine should reconnect. Further research revealed that taking a homeopathic preparation of angel's trumpet could be enough to bridge the gap. The homeopathic version, unlike an actual extract, was generally quite safe. She placed an order and it would be arriving tomorrow.

Turning off the machine, she shuffled to her bedroom, and finished her champagne while watching some of Dr. Lev's latest online posts. She found his teachings and methods of enslavement so empowering.

Day Eleven

"The night enjoys bringing pain to the wise ruler."
Aeschylus

At home, Daemon awakened refreshed and with calm resolve to continue his quest. He intensified his meditation practice. Light channeled not only through his body but through thoughts and sounds. A tangible field of power emanated from him. He let go of any concern about the shutdown, as it actually allowed him more peace and quiet to pursue his quest. The legal entanglement would eventually unravel and resolve.

Having taken his first extract of the day, both his physical and mental energy level increased. He moved smoothly and effortlessly to explore the garden for its latest version of heavenly sustenance. On his way, he decided to check in on Cyndra.

After knocking on the door, he paused, then called her name. While waiting for a response, he looked in the nearby living room window with its typical open blinds. She wasn't on the couch. He walked around the side to check the bedroom window. Those blinds were also open, and there she was, in bed sleeping. *Probably up all night with her phone. She needed her rest.* He left quietly toward his plant harvesting adventure.

Sunlight slivered through the green canopy, as he entered his garden of consciousness. The pounding of a pileated woodpecker echoed the pulse of life through the forest and all its inhabitants. Daemon's heart pumped with the strength and steadiness of his desire for a new life. Like a shamanic vision quest, he explored a deeper level of knowing.

Maneuvering through Schisandra vines, he picked their coveted five flavored fruits, resembling clusters of small red grapes. His eyes softly closed in gratitude for their abundance. Trudging into wetlands, he bowed down humbly, and harvested gotu kola leaves that blanketed the moist soil. Standing at the water's edge, reaching out, fully stretching, he gathered blue lotus, a blossoming of expanded mind. Daemon moved seamlessly; stacking nootropics in his desire to construct a bridge to Utopia, to his own salvation.

Back at the lab he began drying and processing the herbs. Afterwards, he explored the virtual version of his living world. Chemical analysis programs did their best to make sense of his garden's fertile creativity. Unheard of chemical formulas appeared on the monitor. They combined all manner of actions; adaptogen, stimulant, sedative, trace amounts of psychedelics, and more.

While processing the information, he sensed another presence. Swiveling around in his office chair, he saw Cyndra, wearing dark glasses, and holding a bottle of Energeia Nectar. She appeared more like an apparition, quiet and washed out.

"Wow, didn't hear you come in," said Daemon. "Glad to see you're awake."

"I'm more awake than ever," she replied in a low, hoarse tone.

"What's with the shades?"

"Feeling sensitive to light today." She spoke in a matter of fact way.

"You seem more pale than usual, and you sound different. Are you feeling ok?" His eyebrows raised with genuine curiosity.

"Fine." She drank down the nectar like it was fruit juice.

"The way you're downing that Energeia, you might be feeling hyper fine." He tried to express some levity, to break up her unnerving strangeness.

"All I have left to drink are nectars. How about something else?"

"Sure, what can I get you?"

"Two cases of bottled water."

"Two cases? You know you're only going to be here a few more days. Your Aunt Lynette should be back then."

"Good," she said, throwing the empty nectar bottle in a trash can.

"Cyndra, as usual, you're either amazing or baffling."

With hands on her hips, she cleared her gravelly voice and said, "I'm thirsty."

"Got it. I know you like your water cold," he said as he headed to the refrigerator. It was some effort carrying that much water from the lab to the guest house, but Daemon figured he could use some strength building exercise. Finishing the delivery, he promptly returned to the lab.

As Daemon printed out some documents, he

received a call from Mara.

"Just wanted to say goodbye," she said.

"Oh, okay. Glad to hear you're leaving," Daemon replied.

"No, I'm not leaving. You are."

"I'm locked in, remember? Not going anywhere." He leaned back in the chair.

Mara paused, then said, "Have you ever wondered what you would do if today was your last day on earth?"

"Not really."

"Maybe you should."

"Is that a threat?"

"I would say it's just good advice."

Daemon's eyes narrowed as he put the phone down. He stood up and stepped outside for some fresh air, then proceeded down the driveway toward his house. In the distance he could see the sheriff's car still parked at the entrance. Changing his point of view, he turned and walked up to his home. Once inside, he realized it was lunchtime, and blended up some fruit and honey. The smoothie helped soothe his nerves.

Afterwards, walking back to the lab, Daemon spied Cyndra sitting along the edge of the driveway, in a sunny spot near her house. Definitely a red flag, to see her sitting in the hot sun, of her own volition. He meandered over to investigate.

"Don't mind me asking but, have you been taking drugs or something? You're just not yourself," Daemon stated.

"What? You've got to be dreaming," she said, "I'm totally in the real world; more aware than ever," she

182

said.

"While observing the *real* world, are you aware of the *real* fire ant mound right in front of you?"

"Of course, that's why I'm here. Feeding them mango." She pulled a small piece of juicy, golden fruit out of a plastic container, and gently placed it on the ant's earthy home. The tiny inhabitants scrambled out and soon began feeding. "They're not so bad. More like some misunderstood version of sweet, little sugar ants." She sipped some water. "They prefer sunny areas, don't they?"

"That's right." Daemon smiled. It was unreal; she actually liked things he liked, things everyone else hated. A sense of his transformational ability as an instructor rose up within, only to quickly crash into the more sobering thought that her behavior was too far removed from normal. *Something was wrong, but what?*

"They like to eat sweets, but also flesh," she said, this time adding a piece of cooked chicken onto the animated mound.

"They clean up everything," he said, leaning in for a closer look.

She looked at him and said, "Including the evil in this garden."

"What evil?" he asked, his eyebrows raised.

"The evil that's hidden inside shadow." She adjusted her dark glasses. "Looking deeply into darkness can be illuminating."

"Of course." Daemon nodded, familiar with the Jungian concept of shadow, yet perplexed by her preoccupation with evil, coupled with the odd behavior.

183

"Hope you've still got something to treat bites in case your miniature friends turn on you."

"I don't think it's me that they're going to turn on."

Back in the lab, Daemon cooled off, and let go of Cyndra's disturbing behavior. It could be something trivial, especially at her age. He experimented with another extract and tracked the analysis on his computer. While doing that, he caught up with Lynette on the phone.

"As you asked, I'm going over the financials for Psi-Matics Global," said Lynette. "There's so much disturbing activity, it's mind numbing. Psi-Matics has been irradiating supplements using technology that's pretty questionable. They have all kinds of ties to deep state global initiatives. A legal investigation is going on, but a well-connected organization like that has lots of protection."

"I knew you'd find plenty."

"In addition, there was a curious purchase recently delivered directly to her residence. It's from Infinity Inverts, a Guatemalan company that supplies live insects, tarantulas, and the like. She ordered 200 Manduca occulta, cocoon stage. I looked it up; they're moths."

"So, that's where they came from... Mara," he said, easing himself down on a chair. "Lynette, they're all over my property."

"Wow, that's odd."

"What's Mara up to?" Daemon's mind raced into many conspiratorial directions.

After the revealing conversation with Lynette, Daemon called Katashi. "Did you ever go deeper with the chemical analysis of the extracts?"

"I was just going to call you. Got the results back from my friend Dan, who works with some cutting-edge technology."

"What did he find?"

"He's into epigenetics, and said your extracts caused genes to turn on in ways he hasn't seen before."

"How's that?"

"They activated a much greater number of genes than any supplement or drug he has ever tested."

"Is that a good thing?"

"He wasn't sure, but believes that if someone wanted more transformation in their life, this would be the way to go."

"That's what I'm looking for," said Daemon.

"There's one other thing. He ran it through a program that estimates the length of time that the effects would continue. It was unclear how long the results would last. It could be long lasting."

"That sounds awesome, a permanent change for the better," Daemon replied.

Katashi's tone shifted. "If it's a permanent change, let's hope it *is* for the better."

After the call, Daemon considered the genetic change. Was it caused by the new alkaloids and other chemicals his plants produced? Perhaps the parasitic plants facilitated the transmission of viruses, which are all about genetic change. Or, it could be something more obscure, like vortex energy. The questions kept coming as he jotted down a few notes for further inquiry.

Daemon called Shavonda just to see how she was doing. He missed her capabilities in the lab, and her jovial nature.

"Hope you've been enjoying your vacation," Daemon said.

"I miss being there. You're probably loving the alone time," Shavonda said, with a chuckle.

"It's okay. My lawyer says the shutdown should be overturned in a day or two, and I've made progress on the nectar."

"Great, I have faith you'll succeed. I see the trolls are still yacking about the toads."

"Most people don't know any better. The media is whipping people up into eco-terrorists."

"That's the media we know and love," she said with some snark. "How's Cyndra?"

"That's a good question. Lately, she's been acting more peculiar than usual. I'm getting concerned about her, she's become a different person."

"Maybe all that transformational energy you've got going on there is helping her to change," said Shavonda.

"I don't think it's a change for the better."

After the call, Daemon speculated whether Cyndra's odd behavior derived from the nectars. She was taking so much of them lately. Could this be a long lasting effect on her? Mara's criticism of his work crept back to haunt him. *Am I really doing the right thing?*

Despite the possibility of unknown consequences, he persevered. With so much momentum for his quest, moving forward was the only option. Observing the latest results, his heart rhythms synced up with his brain waves. His compassion for Cyndra deepened. It also extended to the rest of his crew. He allowed himself to truly feel deep appreciation for others.

Curious about Armando, he called to touch base with him.

"Good to hear from you, Daemon," said Armando.

"Watch out, all this down time is going to soften you up," Daemon said.

"I need to come back to work," he replied. "It's easier than dealing with the wife and kids all day."

"I'm doing all the harvesting myself. I don't know how you routinely perform so much work. Feels like one more day of this and I'm going to die," said Daemon, and laughed.

After sharing with his friends, Daemon felt more opened up. He stepped outside and sat down on the walkway. Leaning back against the exterior wall, under an overhang, he watched the sky.

Clouds coalesced, thickening the sky. Strong sunlight dimmed and diffused behind smoky black titan clouds. Spacious blue portals shrunk and disappeared in the gathering density. Currents of air blew and rolled through his medicinal forest in waves. Branches vacillated and stretched in the cleansing flow, releasing dead leaves and debris. Cool air smoothed over Daemon as he opened to the elements. A piercing light ripped the sky, splitting atmospheric nitrogen, that nourished plants. He took a deep breath of the fertile air. The scorching bolts seared oxygen into ozone. The sweet, pungent scent cleansed his being. Thunder ricocheted through the landscape and resonated through his bones. Rain spat and pattered on the foliage. The pace accelerated; it became a roaring blur. Daemon brimmed with the vigor of life. He rose up with ease and proceeded inside the lab, to look more deeply within. How could he bring the life enhancing power of storm energy into his work?

Mara received the delivery of her homeopathic angel's trumpet. Ready for tonight, she enjoyed some champagne, and called her granddaughter Zyla. "How are things in Nepal?" she asked.

"Summering here is totally refreshing," said Zyla.

"I'm jealous, but things should be wrapping up shortly, then I'll be back home in London."

"I've heard the investigation into Psi-Matics turned into a lawsuit. Will we be okay?"

"Don't worry, we've got connections all over the world. It's not going anywhere."

"Okay, good. Trying not to worry. Just want some down time before going back to work at the ashram in Kerala."

"How's the research going?"

"You really picked an amazing place, there's no end to the caverns, and the sound quality is mind blowing."

"Dr. Lev helped me discover that spot. He seems to

know everything." She continued to catch up on her granddaughter's life, and finally drew the conversation to a close with promises to see each other soon.

Next, Mara went online to make sure the cane toad protests were still active. She checked with El Dorado's notices, confirming the boycott of Elysium Jungle. Looking at the controlled substance charge against Elysium; she smiled as Daemon and Cyndra were still trapped like rats. Lifting a glass to toast her own accomplishment she spoke out loud, "Elysium and it's portal will soon be mine." Finishing off her drink, she called Dr. Lev before it got too late.

"Nothing like Florida in the summer," said Lev with wryness.

"Fortunately, I should be finishing this assignment shortly, and returning to England."

"Has your excursion into plant medicines been fruitful?"

"We've downloaded tons of information on new botanical substances and their effects on consciousness and behavior."

"Are you working with the moths?"

"Yes, they've added a whole new dimension to artificial intelligence. Also, as the A.I. creates a stronger connection, I should be able to more fully direct the moths' activity." Mara enjoyed sharing information with her mentor. Finding a point of completion, she gave her farewell and returned to tonight's preparations.

Hovering over the tree line, the egg yolk colored moon began the gestation of night. As darkness fell around the lab, Daemon's face was aglow from his computer. He layered the neural effect of one extract onto another, assembling his utopian puzzle. While scrolling through the information, the sensation of being watched came over him. It reminded him of Cyndra eerily observing him earlier. he turned and sure enough, outside the window there she was, with her gaze fixed on him. *This is crazy.* Daemon rose up and stepped outside to see what she wanted.

Cyndra stood in a pool of moon light, covered with occult sphinx moths. Some hung onto her white dress with their silver grey wings neatly folded. Others buzzed around her; their flittering wings revealing moon-like abdominal spots. One hand clenched a small purse, and the other a glass bottle. She stared at Daemon with dark eyes, framed by a face with a bleached out soul. "Daemon, the moths are mad at you." She brushed one of them gently away from her face. "You cut down all the angel's trumpets; their favorite food." Lifting the small bottle to her lips, she emptied its contents.

"Cyndra, what's up with the moths? Are you wearing honey or some special oil? he asked.

"No, it's just me. I'm their new angel's flower," she said, caressing one on her chest. "They love me... unlike some people." She tossed the empty bottle at him.

Daemon snapped it out of the air. "That's Eros Nectar. What are you doing, chugging it like that?"

"I'm having an intimate relationship with the night," she said, and puckered her lips toward the yellow disk floating in the dark sky. She pulled her hair back, while hovering moths shadowed her movements.

"Cyndra, something's wrong. I don't mean to sound critical, but maybe you should do some testing in the lab. I say that because I really care about you." His gaze alternated between her ghostly appearance and the fuzzy night sprites.

"This is what you really care about." She reached toward the ground, simultaneously setting down her purse, and grabbed a large cane toad well camouflaged with the dirt. Lifting the wriggling and squirming creature, her slender arms fully flexed. In defense, the toad's paratoid glands began to secrete a creamy white cocktail of drugs onto her skin.

"I'd be careful, the toads here are more potent than usual." Daemon recalled an accusation of him feeding them psychedelic plants to make them more toxic. Not far from the truth.

Cyndra stepped toward Daemon, holding the warty creature close to his face. "If it wasn't for your toads, my Nisha would still be alive." Her black eyes expanded, reflecting the moon.

"Nisha's dead? I'm sorry, I didn't know…"

"How could you? Always wrapped up in your own world." She threw the seeping animal down, and it promptly leapt away. Rubbing her hands together, she massaged the bewitching ointment deeper into her skin.

"Seriously Cyndra, you shouldn't do that," he said, shaking his head.

"There you go, ordering people around like sheep." Her fingers sticking together, as she rubbed farther up her forearms. "This stuff really gets my heart pumping."

"I'm trying to look out for your best interests."

"All you look out for are your own selfish interests. Stop the madness, Daemon." She reached down, picked up her purse, and pulled out the gift from Mara. Holding up the half empty bottle, she announced, "This nectar destroyed my beautiful illusions. Truth is devastating, but magical. Now I see the evil," she said, handing him the receptacle, "and now I have the power to destroy it."

Daemon cautiously received the bottle from Cyndra. He looked at it and said, "Is this a joke? I didn't make this." His shoulders lifted. "And, what's this evil you keep referring to?"

"Daemon, the pretense is over," she said, waving her arm. "I must go, I have a date with my shadow lover." She turned toward the dense forest. Stepping away from the pool of lunar light, she and her blurry winged friends disappeared into the jungle shade.

Inside the lab, Daemon prepared the liquid for the mass spectrometer, and submitted it. The machine went through its chemical decoding. The identified chemicals came up on the screen. Scopolamine, atropine, and the list continued with other tropane alkaloids. Plant source: angel's trumpet. Daemon gasped. He didn't want to believe it, but this explained her odd appearance and behavior. The bottle did look convincing, even the font type was the same. Someone went to a lot of trouble to create a simulation of his products, but with deadly contents. *It had to have been Mara. But why?*

Daemon immediately began creating an antidote for angel's trumpet intoxication. A little research enabled him to come up with a list of ingredients. He needed a cholinesterase inhibitor; wild lettuce could provide that. A benzodiazepine would be helpful; he could get that from artemisia. He rounded out the mix with a few other therapeutic plants. Daemon expressed a sigh of relief after finding all the extracts that he needed already there at his lab. He blended and completed his fix for a bad trip, and went out to find Cyndra.

Opening her front door, he stepped in and called for her. After exploring each room to no avail, he exited into the garden. He called again, and still no response, straining to listen over the sounds of the night. Before long, the futility became apparent and he left, to resume his search first thing tomorrow. *Where is she, and what is she doing?*

From the shadows, Cyndra observed Daemon returning home, like an owl watching a rat. *He thinks he can find me? He's so stupid. I'll show him who's in control.* His house lights turned off, signaling her to move. She hastened to the lab. At the entrance, she uncovered the spare key hidden under a rock, and entered. With her recently acquired night vision, she left the lights off. Stepping into the production room, she rummaged through the product labels. Finding the one for passionflower honey, she took it and visited the toxic honey cabinet. Pulling open a drawer for the key, she unlocked the wooden doors. Reaching inside, she retrieved the yellow jasmine honey. Locking everything back, she returned home.

Sitting on her couch, she lit one candle, more than enough light for detailed work. Unscrewing the lid on the honey jar, she raised it to her nose, and deeply inhaled it's bouquet of sinister sweetness. Returning the lid, she removed the yellow jasmine label, and relabeled it passion flower honey.

She opened a bottle of Energeia Nectar and guzzled it down. A loud sound erupted over the other night creatures; the wailing of coyotes. Their screaming sounded almost human as apparently, they had made a kill. She had a new found appreciation for the natural balance of life; the need for predator and prey.

The sounds drew her outside into the night jungle. She followed the entrancing frequencies deep into the dark world. External sounds as well as internal thoughts moved her. She heard the voices of both her father and Daemon. They spoke in unison, "I love you, Cyndra." She felt nauseous, yet kept going. Her vision blurred, and her eyelids fluttered. She began to sweat. Dizziness made her stop for a moment. Then anger rose up and pushed all other sensations aside. Her lips grew thin and her hands tightened into fists. Her whole body flexed into battle ready mode. A flurry of punches exploded into empty air as she tried to strike down the imagined threat. She wished to rid her life of Daemon, for pretending to love her, for the death of her cat, for misleading everyone.

Incinerated from her fiery outburst, she slowed down and caught her breath. She came upon an upland area, with spineless prickly pear cactus. Eating the fruit, soft and mucilaginous, it soothed her dry mouth and lips. Her nausea went away, and her blood pressure lowered. She continued with her journey, passing by the soft, organic geometry of foliage, cast in silvery light. Night sounds echoed harmoniously, until the screaming of a peacock overpowered everything. A surprisingly scary voice for such a beautiful bird; it may have been calling for a mate. Cyndra thought it possibly shocked its partner into submission. She traveled more deeply into the night forest, toward the center, all the way to the spawning pool.

The pool was wide, yet relatively shallow, maybe waist or chest high at the deepest. A variety of plants hugged the shoreline. Just beyond these, purple and white trumpet flowers of water datura spread open wide for visiting moths. These small cousins to angel's trumpets contributed their similar essences to the pool.

The water quivered from the toad's vigorous courtship. They bobbed and entangled with each other. The males on the backs of females, wrapped their arms around them, locking themselves in place. Their penetrating calls drowned out Cyndra's extraneous thoughts or feelings.

Sweaty and limp, she striped down, tied her hair up, and stepped into the water. The pond needed no mechanized water circulation or fountains, as the abundant rain and plethora of plants filtered and freshened the water. Although not stagnant, it could still involve risk, as it was pharmacologically active due to its squirmy inhabitants. Her feet found their way along the sandy bottom. Cyndra breathed easier, maneuvering through the cool water. She didn't seem to mind the toads like she used to. It wasn't their fault they were here; it was Daemon's. He should know better. The toads were basically nature's creatures, doing whatever they naturally do.

As she explored farther and deeper, her legs swooshed through the enlivening liquid, brushing against the indulgent amphibians. When the water level reached her waist, she eased herself down into a gentle swim. Keeping her head above water, she maintained vigilance as well as some semblance of hygiene. The cool water elicited a smile, and she felt even more weightless than before, if that was possible. She glided along islands of lily pads with pale flowers resembling splashed moonlight. Undulating farther out, she generated a small wake. Her body surged ahead, outlined in glimmering ripples, as she headed for the more open midpoint of the pond. In the absolute center of the garden, her feet relaxed down to the bottom. Upright and balanced, she stood at the powerful focal point of the garden, the center of the vortex. She channeled the diverse life frequencies surrounding her, equally in all directions, and felt completely empowered.

Refreshed and energized, she propelled herself back to shore. Stepping out of the water, chill bumps covered her wet body. She brushed herself off with her hands, and shook her body. Warming back up to normal, and dry enough to don her dress, she prepared to leave. Bursting with energy, she dashed down the path. Although barefoot, she hardly felt the matted leaves. Guided by keen night vision, she avoided all obstacles.

Leaving the jungle, she spied Daemon's house directly ahead. She slowed and quieted her movement, coming into close proximity to his dark house. Tiptoeing toward the bedroom window, she came close enough to see inside. He laid in bed asleep, completely vulnerable. She indulged in what could possibly happen to him in this state. Angry thoughts and feelings revolved through her over and over. Eventually, this madness spiraled out of energy. She turned and slowly ambled home, knowing that tomorrow things would be drastically different.

Cyndra laid on her bed as the outside trills and whistles carried her into another dimension, that of sleep.

The shrill calls of insects escalated to an even higher pitch. They fused and focused, creating a laser beam of sound. This potent transmission penetrated deeply into Cyndra's mind. As if moving through a prism, the beam split into a spectrum of light and sensations. Sinfully indulgent waves rippled through her. This ultrasonic energy carried light, emotions, and even words. Out of this feverishly vibrational space came a shrill message. *Cyndra, open up and flow, you are my nectar*

Mara's face glowed from the image of Cyndra's sleeping form illuminated on her monitor. Sipping champagne spiked with homeopathic angel's trumpet, she maintained her optimal frequency coherence with the target in her sights. She explored the settings on her device, looking to stimulate a greater discharge of life energy from her mark, and consequently give herself a much needed and deserved dose of immortalizing vitality. In addition to encoding her voice commands in a normal frequency range, she added a high frequency range. Each frequency level targeted certain levels of perception. Ultrasonic went deeper into the brain, powerfully stimulating neurotransmitters, hormones and a chemical cascade that released pure life energy. Tonight, Mara was anticipating a blast of young primal energy that would make her feel 20 again.

She clicked the controls, turning them up, and pumped Cyndra's brain with pure eroticism. She opened the channel to allow Cyndra's experience and energy to come in to her. Her eyelids lowered and a smile spread across her face. "Cyndra, you're mine. Your nectar is mine." Cyndra's vital signs rose, but the device had the capacity to keep her asleep and receptive despite increased bodily stimulation.

Mara's vital signs were going up as well. Her breathing became more rapid and shallow, while her eyes shifted to a misty sea green. Tingling spread through her fingers and toes. Internal fans hissed as the machine exerted more power. *Give me your nectar Cyndra. Give it up.* Mara's belly pulsed. She released a ghastly scream, then softened down into the chair. With vital signs returning to normal, she took a few breaths from her inhaler. She glowed from the orgasmic energy boost siphoned off from Cyndra.

Inside Daemon's home, he slept soundly, as his inner world came alive. He dreamed of himself in meditation, observing breathing and cultivating his awareness. Azarias appeared before him, and asked, "Are you dreaming or are you awake?"

This prompted him into more full awareness; cognizant that he was dreaming. In this lucid dream, Daemon decided to seek the answer to Utopia Nectar. Surprisingly, Cyndra appeared before him, holding a glass jar.

"I possess your Utopia Nectar," she said. Unscrewing the lid, a column of dark smoke rose fluidly out of it. It continued, snaking itself through the air toward Daemon. "This will trigger its activation, then you must deeply assimilate it."

The smoke slowly swirled around him, rising up toward his head. The dense suffocating plumes completely shrouded his body, and generated an angry storm within him. Unable to breathe, he fell to the ground. Feeling his life drain away, he wondered, *where's the utopia?*

Daemon gasped, and abruptly sat up in bed. The dream seemed too vivid and real. The transformational energy of death haunted him. *That felt like more than just a dream.*

Day Twelve

"Death is the healer of incurable diseases."
Aeschylus

At the apex of its yearly journey, the sun rose with great authority. Its unyielding force remade everything in its path. Elysium Jungle effervesced with a surplus of life. Pollinators milked the sweet essence of sumptuous botanicals. A flurry of noisy black birds swooped into the new day. Toads relished their breakfast fare, ingesting malachite butterflies and mud dauber wasps.

Cyndra woke up to a pounding on her door. She donned her shades and drifted to the entrance. Daemon stood with a concerned look, holding a small glass bottle labeled antidote.

"I analyzed the contents of your Utopia Nectar. It's angel's trumpet, concentrated and deadly. Your altered state of mind could last for days or even weeks."

"I don't know what you're talking about." She spoke in deep, gravelly tones; a surreal contrast to her delicate form. "All I know is it worked, and I'm in a far better state of mind."

"Mara gave that to you, didn't she?" His eyes flared.

"She exposed you. I can finally see what's really going on." The morning sun glared off of her dark glasses.

"Cyndra, you're not making any sense." He held up the bottle. "I have something that will neutralize the adverse effects."

"Not interested."

"Either you take the antidote or you'll have to leave, today."

"The police are out there." Her head slowly turned side to side. "I don't think that's possible."

"Tell them whatever you have to...you can't stay here like you are now, the effects on your behavior are too unpredictable. Ask them to take you to a hospital." His eyes softened. "I'm sorry."

"You're the one who's not having a sane conversation." She folded her arms. "I have nowhere to go. Can't you wait just another day for aunt Lynette?"

"This is non-negotiable. At some point in the future, when you're feeling better, we can have a talk about... whatever. But not now. This is about safety for both of us."

"Alright then," Cyndra growled. "I'll be ready around noon."

"Fine." Daemon took off for the lab.

Cyndra watched as he walked away and disappeared inside the building. She grabbed the jar labeled passionflower honey, and ventured out. Circling around unnoticed on a path with plenty of overgrowth, she moved stealthily toward Daemon's house. At his entrance, she reached under a rock, got the key, and unlocked the front door. Inside his house she crept into the kitchen. Reaching into a cabinet, she removed his unopened, next in line, jar of honey. Replacing it with hers, she wiped off any fingerprints. As a little insurance policy, she unplugged his Wi-Fi modem and hid it in a drawer. She withdrew out the front door, locked it, and fled back to her house.

Cyndra had several hours before her agreed upon departure time. Packing her clothes, she set aside a special outfit for today. She indulged in a lengthy shower with deliciously scented soaps and shampoo. Fragrant vapor drifted throughout the house. Afterward, she styled her hair with gel; drawing it back into spikes. Along-side her temples, she clamped on the black, pointy hair pins resembling horns. Precious oils enlivened her body. Sucking down Energeia Nectar and listening to gothic rock, she pulsed with dark passion. Cyndra viewed herself in the mirror. She desired to appear as irresistible to Daemon as possible, in order to more easily lure him to whatever she desired. Dark mascara along with her black eyes, increased the dramatic look. Thinking of his seduction, her crimson lips glimmered with a wicked smile. Black fingernails adorned her hands as she reached for her bewitching attire.

Her fragrant, naked body slid into a lacy, black mini dress. One of Mara's seductive gifts, it revealed much more than it covered up. Her mirror reflected a provocative and powerful image. She stepped into black sneakers and continued to dance to dark wave music. Cyndra looked at the time and set her phone down. Putting on sunglasses, she stepped outside with a light gracefulness fueled with dark power. Daemon's ecosystem needed to be harmonized, and for her that meant invoking the balancing power of predator and prey.

She strutted over to the lab, and from a window watched Daemon working. Like a cat watching a mouse, she remained quietly hidden yet vigilant. After a while, he got up and exited the building, heading home. Cyndra jumped into action, going into the lab, pulling out the modem plug and hiding it inside a cabinet. She then proceeded to Daemon's house.

"Cyndra? Is that really you?" Daemon flushed. Although angry, he was nevertheless overwhelmed by her exquisite body wrapped in ephemeral lace. "You look amazing. That's one dangerous dress."

"Just wanted to look presentable," she said.

"Your hairstyle, so sleek and energetic," he said, managing to notice something above her chest.

"I'd really love to stay. Won't you change your mind?"

"Umm, only if you knock that poison out of your system." The instinctual lure toward Cyndra challenged his resolve. Her fragrance brought chills all over his body. He wanted to give in.

Cyndra stepped forward. "Well, if I have to go, is it possible to get some of your amazing honey to take with me. It would mean so much."

Naturally impressed by her interest in his favorite indulgence, Daemon couldn't refuse. "Okay, come in." Inside the kitchen, he reached into a cabinet and pulled out an unopened jar labeled passion flower honey.

"Oh, that new jar is more than I need, plus, I prefer the milder flavor of acacia honey."

"Well, okay, here you go." He handed her the half empty jar of acacia honey, and set the passion flower out on the counter, while almost drooling at her half naked body.

"This morning has flown by, can't believe it's lunch time already," she said, drinking some water. "Having a smoothie?"

"Uh… yes, that's right." His trembling hands pulled out some leaves and fruit from his refrigerator. He realized Cyndra must be trying to seduce him in order to stay, but knowing the potential danger strengthened his resolve. He chopped up the produce and dropped it in his blender. Holding the jar of passion flower honey, he unscrewed the lid, and poured it into the mix.

"Honey is the best part. More is better, isn't it?" she said, licking her lips.

"You did learn a few things here." He added more of the viscous sweetener. Taking a deep breath, he attempted to stay focused. Fully triggered, images of making passionate love to Cyndra scorched his mind. After blending, he took a sip. "Wow, that's really sweet. I don't remember the passion flower being so…hmm, it's hard to describe." He considered the possibility that her unbelievably sweet fragrance influenced his sense of taste.

"You've got so much change going on in the garden, it's remarkable that there's any kind of consistency." She adjusted her short dress, as if it even mattered considering it's revealing quality.

"Good point." He drank with the hope that food could act as some distraction from his rising desire.

"Oh, I took a short walk around this morning, since it's my last day and all. I saw a really large black snake,

I guess it was an indigo, but it had red spots all over it."

"Red spots, that's odd. Where was it?"

"In an open area towards the Sales Center. It was just a few minutes ago. Want to check it out?"

"There's too much to do," he said, shaking his head.

"It could be a new mutation from the effects of your garden."

"Well okay, just a quick look." He finished his smoothie, and followed her out.

Cyndra lead Daemon on a path to an area about midway from his house to the Sales Center. It was a small, relatively open area with low growing perennials surrounded by forest.

"I saw the snake over there," she said, pointing and looking interested.

"Daemon bent over and pushed plants out of his way and kept searching. "Cyndra, be extra careful around the bees, you're wearing so much essential oil." Moving about, a headache began to pound in the front of his head. He rarely had headaches, and chalked it up to his recent overwork. Trudging through the vegetation, he strained his eyes for the snake. "Cyndra, I don't think there's anything here."

"I'm sure it's here, and it's so huge it can't stay hidden for long." She reached her arms out to their maximum extension.

Daemon continued on, and cleared his throat. "I wish I had brought something to drink, my throat is so dry."

"Here, take some of my water." Cyndra handed him her bottle.

"Thanks," he said, then taking a long drink, "that's

better." He returned the bottle to her. "I think I should get back to the lab."

"No! I mean… just a few more minutes. I'd love to get a photo of that snake to post online. Otherwise, no one would believe how fantastic your wildlife is."

"Just one more minute," he said, as he noticed his legs and arms becoming heavy and awkward. His head continued to pound as he searched further. "Cyndra, I'm suddenly feeling like, I don't know, extremely tired."

"No wonder, you've been working day and night. Just relax a moment, take a few deep breaths. You know how good that is."

Daemon paused, and focused on his breathing. "Good suggestion." After a few moments, he turned his head for one more search, but he almost fell down. "Wow, I'm so dizzy."

"You should sit down and rest for a moment. Here's a clear space, you can lean back on that tree stump." Cyndra took Daemon's arm and guided him down to a more restful position on the ground.

"Something is definitely wrong. My body feels so stiff. I can barely move." He managed to pull his phone out of his pocket and turned it on. The phone became difficult to hold, his hands numb. He tried to dial emergency, but his fingers fumbled, hitting more numbers than he meant to.

"Having trouble?" she said casually.

"Trying to call Emergency," he stammered, his hands becoming less mobile. "I need help… please dial it for me."

"You bet I'll take your phone." She snatched it out of

Daemon's incapacitated hand.

Daemon did not hear her making the call. He managed to crank his head slightly to the side, attempting to see her. "Make the call. Now!" He labored to get the muffled words out. "Cyndra..." he took a breath, "dial...the..." his mouth and throat exhausted, "numb..." Daemon had lost his ability to speak.

"Remember Daemon, it's not a good idea to use your phone in the garden, it interferes with your connection to nature." She stepped carefully around him, like a vulture circling around an incapacitated animal.

Daemon strained his eyes but couldn't move them. They were now set in place, looking straight ahead. Trapped in this position, his mind strained even more than his body. He was completely paralyzed. *Paralyzed from what?*

"You can't move a muscle," she said, and tilted an ear toward him, "but I can hear those gears turning inside your head." She adjusted her sunglasses. "Just another piece of the puzzle, isn't it?" Sipping some water, she observed him for a moment.

Although he couldn't move his eyes, he could still see out of them, as long as his eyelids stayed open. He could hear and sense everything, just unable to move. He pondered his fate. *What did Cyndra want? Was escape possible? Am I going to die?* His breathing became more shallow, his stomach tightened in knots. He tried to keep panic at bay.

"If you can't use your phone in paradise, what good is it?" She reached her arm back, then heaved the phone through the air. It disappeared into a thicket. "Got any other goodies in your pants?" She bent down and slid her hands into his pockets and felt around. "Hmm, nothing here but the usual junk." She stood up, and surveilled the situation. A few bees hovered around some flowers. On either side of Daemon sat fire ant mounds. "Daemon, I know a lot of people don't appreciate fire ants, but thank God you do."

She broke off a long, stiff plant stem, and stuck it into the ant mounds. "Sometimes they need a little wake up call." The ants poured out of the mounds. They crawled on the ground around Daemon, then onto his hands and arms. Many of them stopped and pressed themselves close to his skin, injecting venom. "Now that's a shot in the arm. That'll get you going...oops, I forgot, looks like you're practicing stillness and meditation. Aren't you glad you've got those tools for better living?" An obscene smile etched across her lips, as the ants continued their march over Daemon's body. "You're so attuned to nature, embracing the flow of life." The ants spread incessantly, now crawling on his shoulders and neck

To Cyndra, this was the perfect eradication of an evil life. Daemon, dead from the accidental consumption of his own bad medicine. Case closed. She stood over him, enveloped in an aura of flowery oils.

A bee began to hover around her. She swished it away, but it persisted, buzzing around her face. She waved her arms to no avail. Finally, her hands slapped together, crushing the bee. She managed to do it without getting stung, and her lips widened with a self-congratulatory smile. She stood triumphant for a moment, until another bee showed up. Then another flew in, and more kept coming, escalating into a swarm. Frantically swatting them away, her heart beat quickened. The buzzing grew louder; a deep, angry droning. They stung her arms and hands. Her muscles tensed and quivered. They attacked her chest, neck, and face. Pain shot throughout her body. Her arms flailed helplessly. She shrieked and began running to the nearest building, the Sales Center. Suffering dozens of stings, her breathing became labored. Feeling nauseous and faint, she thrust the door open, entered, and managed to slam it behind her, before passing out onto the floor.

Daemon's skin burned, stung, and itched. The ants began their most deadly trek into his nose and mouth. Fending off extreme fear and rage, he focused deeply, and managed to shift his awareness away from his impending doom. Bees flew within his field of vision, giving him an idea on how to stop the ants. Recalling his internal mantra practice, he could influence the bees with mental tones. He imitated their short, intermittent pulses of buzzing sound within his head. Remembering the teachings of Azarias, that the internal sound of our minds affected the external environment, much more than we realized. Visualizing the ants being removed, he empowered the mantra with intention. He didn't want to exit this world yet, there were so many goals left to attain.

The Africanized bees hovered closer to him. They

began to land on his body, attacking the fire ants. The bees used their jaws to bite and crush the cantankerous dirt dwellers. Although ants generally ruled the insect world, killer bees can be quite formidable, especially in the right numbers. Daemon kept up the mantra, and the bees kept coming. A dark, buzzing cloud descended, as countless warring insects blanketed him. They locked mandibles with each other. The ant's stingers probed in every direction, attempting to find vulnerable spots on the bees. The crawling sensations on his body seemed endless. Daemon lost all track of time, yet managed to keep his attention on the world of sound. The battle progressed, and the number of ants dwindled. The bees buzzed fiercely as many of the ants retreated back to their dark, underground bases. Daemon's mantra resonated through his bones. It blurred out the stinging agony of his body

Although riddled with anguish and rage, he channeled that energy into a more purposeful path. Utilizing the pillar of light meditation, he connected with the heavens. Projecting his electromagnetic energy field into that spacious realm, he visualized light streaking down. He transformed his internal storm into an external storm.

White shimmering clouds lost their luster. Like a growing shadow, they shifted to charcoal grey and black. Cool wind blew on the remaining insects, signaling them all to take cover. Lightning crashed around him. Completely exposed, his only consolation being that he was the lowest spot on the landscape. Rain rattled the foliage, bowing it down under the pummeling force. It washed away all traces of crawling life forms. Daemon transitioned from baking to freezing, but thankfully, it numbed the painful stings, and refreshed his mind. Once the rain drenched everything, the storm left as quickly as it came.

In this wet world, he now called the cane toads. Favoring moist environments, they naturally ventured out after a storm. In his mind, he mimicked their mating calls. Out from the soggy vegetation, a large toad plopped near him. Daemon's mind pulsed with the percussive mantra, and more toads appeared out the foliage. Large and small they gathered around him. He felt the weight of their flabby bodies in contact with his hands and arms. They even advanced up to his shoulders and neck.

Daemon's internal mantra pounded more strongly as if it had a life of its own. The amped up amphibians excreted creamy concoctions composed of many drugs including morphine. Soaking into his welt ridden skin, it deeply soothed his pain. The stimulating cardiac glycosides increased his heartbeat and respiration. Despite facing his own mortality, he managed to invoke gratitude for his life. His heart and mind tingled with the challenge to find positive inner growth from even the most horrific circumstances.

He transformed and achieved the long sought after, precious state of transcendent intelligence. His body felt expansive and light; less solid and more vaporous. A sense of rotational movement within his cloudy form became apparent. As thoughts swirled through his mind, so did his increasingly indefinable shape also swirl. It grew into a vortex of movement, like a whirlwind. Mirroring the vortex energy of his garden, he remembered the insight from Azarias concerning its portal quality. Daemon reinvented his ability to wield the forces of nature to effect great change. His tornado-like body blurred with more velocity, recalling the actual whirlwind in his garden over a week ago. His spinning form blackened as mushroom spores flew up from his garden, clouding his vision. Continuing to quietly observe, Mara and Griff's house appeared through the dark mist. The energy slowed, and the mushroom spores rained down around their house. As if watching in time lapse photography, spores grew into mushrooms carpeting their lawn.

Daemon's 'twister' body spun into some electric current. Sparks crackled throughout his energetic field. Visions of the Blackstone's psychotronic equipment came into view. Mara's evil thoughts, propelled by technology, shot through his mind. He became more aware of her plot to destroy him and probably Cyndra in the process. Observing Mara's world, everything became increasingly dark, yet interspersed with blinding bolts of electricity. Smothered with negativity, sparked and jolted, Daemon once again felt the need to change.

He released the compulsive need to create Utopia Nectar. Although it could be a good idea, it did not need to rule his life. Others had hijacked his mind many years ago, programming his obsession to accomplish these things. Recognizing and letting go of thoughts not genuinely his own, he explored deeply into his true nature. Rather than forcing the experience of transcendent intelligence, he allowed it to happen organically.

Daemon awakened more powerfully to his life.

Cyndra's body ached as she lay sprawled on the floor. Her eyes opened to the faint light of sunset coming through the Sales Center window. Realizing she had been unconscious all afternoon, her head spun as she struggled to stand up. She grabbed a bottle of water out of the refrigerator to wet her papery mouth. Exhausted, she downed a few Energeia nectars from the counter. She found some dragon's blood and applied it to the welts all over her body. Some presence of mind returned, as she recovered from anaphylactic shock. *Daemon. What's happening with Daemon?*

Not knowing what to expect, she grabbed a knife out of the breakroom, and staggered out the door. Although her body ached, her one pointed focus kept her moving. Returning to the open field, she found the area with the tree stump. She stood and looked in disbelief. Daemon was gone.

Cyndra surmised he escaped to his house, being fairly close. She pushed herself in that direction. Daemon's dark house blended in with the increasing gloom. The emergency generator running at the lab indicated the power was out, possibly from a storm. She grasped the door handle; it would not turn. It was unlocked when they left earlier today so, he must have returned and locked her out. Finding the spare key, she entered his home.

Inside, she crept toward the glow of wavering

candlelight emanating from his kitchen. She inched into the doorway.

"Not another step," Daemon stammered. He sat at the kitchen table upon which were various bottles of healing extracts and salves. His bumpy, damaged skin glistened with healing ointments. With both hands, Daemon held a Glock pointed directly at her.

"Oh, I didn't know you owned a gun," Cyndra said in broken tones.

"A part of me wants to shoot you right now." Although his voice was weak, his message beamed out.

"I know you couldn't do that, but I understand how you feel. Please, let me explain."

"Tell me everything, and it needs to be the truth."

Cyndra realized this was going to have to be convincing. Her voice dropped down to a lower and more sorrowful tone as she said, "I'm sorry Daemon, this has all been like a nightmare for me."

"Go on," he said quickly.

"I struggle with feeling inadequate. My childhood was a disaster. Aunt Lynette spoke so highly of you. I came here hoping to create a better life." She paused and assessed her strategy. She portrayed herself as a victim who wanted to improve her life by working with Daemon, and complimented him as well. She was confident this would end up going her way.

"Okay, and..."

"I admit I'm very impressionable, and Mara took advantage of that. She said awful things about you. I challenged her, but she was too strong and persuasive. I'm sorry, I didn't know what I was getting into."

"Keep going."

"She even visits me in my dreams. I can't escape her reach." Cyndra thought that was a good touch, as Daemon valued dreams.

"I see, that's something to consider."

Great, I have him reconsidering. "I hold nothing against you for anything you did or didn't do. You've been under tremendous pressure lately. Frankly, I don't know how you do so much."

"Cyndra, this isn't about me, it's about you. If you're so sorry about everything, why not take the antidote?"

Hmmm, I need a stall tactic. "Daemon, I'll feel more like taking it later, after I clean up, and take care of these stings."

"Do it now… I don't want to use this." His tone grew more serious.

"Where is the antidote?" she asked.

"In the lab."

"Okay, let's go." Each additional moment was an opportunity to escape. Cyndra still had her knife, and as she walked in front of Daemon, she wove it through the fish net mesh on the front of her dress.

Daemon guided her out of his house and followed closely as they walked to the nearby lab. Storm clouds crossed the sky, intermittently obscuring the bright moon. The industrial sound of the lab's emergency generator pounded against the organic sounds of the night.

Inside the shadowy lab, flashes of red and green emanated from the offline equipment, signaling to be reset. Because only the lab machinery was hooked up to the generator, all other lights were out.

Cyndra's black dress blended into the darkness. Her pale skin pulsed in and out of the gloom, like warning coloration. She abruptly turned with a kaleidoscopic effect, simultaneously folding her hand with the knife behind her. Facing Daemon, the electronic distress signals highlighted the welts on her face and other areas of her body.

Daemon positioned himself on the other side of the counter facing Cyndra. He kept his equalizer at the ready, and asked, "Are you hiding something behind your back?"

Cyndra's black eyes loomed large at Daemon. She maneuvered her arm behind her, then outstretched both arms. "It's just me." For a moment, she appeared open and responsive. As soon as her arms came down, however, the knife fell, clanging on the floor beneath her.

"That really is a dangerous dress," he said. "Kick away the sharp accessory."

She reluctantly cooperated, slowly pushing it with her shoe, not very far.

"Cyndra, I'm serious. No more fooling around," he demanded.

"Why not? Fooling around with you can be awesome." Her voice became soft and breathy.

"You know what I mean." His gaze narrowed.

"Yes, I know exactly what you mean." She jiggled closer. "Remember the time you rubbed my legs with dragon's blood to soothe the ant stings? Your touch is so amazing." She slid her hands along her sinuous thighs. "You alleviated the pain, and increased my desire." Her tongue caressed her lips.

Daemon stood firm, although delightful memories of Cyndra began to soften him.

"And when we danced, I wanted you even more." Cyndra's hips began to sway. She fondled her abdomen and breasts. Sensuous movement undulated throughout her body.

"Play time is over. The antidote is waiting," he barked. Pouring it into a small glass, he waved his gun toward the sepia colored remedy.

She sighed, and approached the counter. Her dark gaze became more tactile. "You no longer think I'm desirable?"

"That's not it," he said firmly. "You need to get well."

"Okay, it's your loss." Cyndra rolled her eyes, then refocused on Daemon. "You may not desire me as a lover, but I have so much more to offer." The devices continued their urgent blinking. One side of her face strobed scarlet, the other harlequin green.

"What do you mean?" asked Daemon.

"My senses are so heightened; in the dark I see everything." She stared at him, her eyes like bottomless pits. "My hearing is fantastic, it's like I can feel the shape of sounds."

"Your senses are more acute, so what?" he said harshly.

"Daemon, I could take your work to a whole new level. I'm the living embodiment of the night. I can summon up what you can't even see." Her arms floated up and around her. "I breathe the essence of the moon, and its hidden magnetic powers over all living things. With my help, your work will be more fantastic than ever."

Daemon considered what she said; it somehow sounded intriguing. Perhaps incorporating the dark feminine energy into the garden would bring some new perspective to his work. Images flashed through his mind of the garden distilling psychoactive chemicals from moonlight, or simply through Cyndra's presence. Gazing into her eyes, however, he felt her compulsive thoughts, forcefully projected into him. He shuddered from the cold, sinister side of the psychedelic nightshade plants she embodied. Both his mind and body suffocated from the flood of dark desires. Realizing her hypnotic manipulation, he resisted it. His eyes flared as his hold on the gun strengthened. "The only deal is take the antidote or die," he demanded.

Cyndra's expression turned even more frigid and shadowy. Her body tightened. "Even if you kill me, my power will haunt you. It will destroy you."

"You don't scare me." Daemon's stance anchored down as his weapon aimed steadily at her. "I'm counting to three, take the medicine, or I'm pulling the trigger. One…" Cyndra stood defiant. "Two…" Her expression communicated total disbelief that Daemon would ever pull the trigger. "Three…"

Daemon's focus shifted for a moment before the blinding flare of ignition, and loud blast. A red splash covered Cyndra's body. Daemon, at the last moment, had repositioned his aim, and shot a beaker of dragon's blood on the counter near her. Broken glass with blood-colored extract sprawled all over.

"That was a warning. This one is for real." He stretched out his arms, with his hands sweaty against the metal.

Cyndra grabbed the glass.

"One..." spoke Daemon. She slowly lifted the remedy. "Two..." She held it near her lips. "Three..."

A deafening shock wave shook both of them to their core. Simultaneously, a piercing flash shuttered through the window blinds. The sensor lights stopped, as the room went dark. Daemon winced at the smell of burned machinery wafting through the lab. *Lightning must have struck the generator.*

Something splashed Daemon's face. His eyes immediately burned and squeezed shut. His nostrils flared from the alcohol based counteragent. Footsteps pounded away from him, and out the back door to the garden.

Daemon flushed his eyes with water, easing the sting. There had never been any intention of killing or even hurting Cyndra; it was all a bluff. He staggered outside to follow her. With eyes watering, he stepped cautiously through a blurry world. His shoes squished into a carpet of soggy leaves. Trees glowed then darkened as clouds intermittently drafted across the moon. Turbulent night sounds echoed throughout the lush darkness. Ahead, the path split into several directions. *Where would she go?*

His pace slowed to a stop. A warm, wet breeze brought attention to the dance of life surrounding him.

He became more still, closed his eyes, and utilized intuition. Thinking of Cyndra, he simply allowed images to appear. A large, circular body of water came to mind. *She's at the spawning pool.* Following inner guidance, he began the trek to go deep into the murky forest.

Too exhausted to effectively challenge Daemon, Cyndra escaped to restore her strength before their next confrontation, before taking him down... permanently. She stumbled along a slippery trail; her heart pounded along with the percussive beat of the cold blooded denizens of the dark forest. With her energy spent, she pushed onward desperately toward the spawning pool, recalling its deeply restorative quality. Brushing wet branches along the winding pathway, she panted and held her aching side. Around the next curve, the narrow pathway opened up to her watery oasis. Standing near the shore, she bent over for a few moments, catching her breath. The knife she had scooped off the lab floor hung loosely in her hand. Shuffling off her shoes, she stepped into the spawning pool...the pool of life.

Her toes wiggled in the silty bottom, and plenty of support rebounded up from her arches. Her legs moved more effortlessly as they swished around the squirmy animals. Wading out into deeper water, she began to swim. Keeping her head above water, she remained present to her surroundings. Amphibians caressed her body while streaming through this buoyant world. Her face softened and she released a deep sigh. She began to swim in a wide arcing spiral toward the center, savoring the calm, restorative spirit of this special place. Her curving trajectory followed a subtle current, not so much about water, but more like a magnetic pathway. A tingling radiance rolled through her, like the phosphorescence of deep sea life. This energy guided her to the center of the vortex, where she once again found her power spot. Settling down, she stood in water chest high, and closed her eyes. The waves of illuminated aliveness kept spiraling in...filling her. Suspended in the center of life, her spine flowed with vitality, like an iridescent indigo snake, its brilliant rainbows emerging from darkness.

On the adjacent property, the Blackstone's villa stood radiant in the stormy night, with multiple generators grinding out countless kilowatts. Inside, the mechanical noise was muted by a romantic fantasia, piped through every room. Mara gleefully stepped toward her psychotronic sanctuary, while sipping champagne. Once inside, she plopped down in front of the equipment, like a teenager home alone with a video game. Indicator lights flashed on as she powered up the device. Tweaking the frequencies, she maximized the impact of her mind warping instrument. Dialing into her target, the screen lit up with Cyndra's body flowing smoothly through water. Mara's heart beat increased, and her loins tingled. She took another drink, and had her inhaler on standby. Her eyes sparkled lime green as she practiced her own style of positive thinking. *Tonight, Daemon will inhabit the real Elysium...the World of the Dead.*

Mara zoomed out the image of Cyndra for a wider perspective. At the edge of the screen, she spied Daemon inching along near the pond. Her serious gaze contrasted with a devilish grin. It was time to utilize the machine's ability to direct the movement of moths. With a hold on his coordinates, she clicked on the artificial intelligence feature for the flying creatures, sending them in his direction. Across the expanse of his garden, occult sphinx moths altered their flight. They began to flock together, droning toward the garden's center.

With her enhanced night vision, Cyndra had observed Daemon from a fair distance away as he stepped out from the forest and into the area around the lake. This gave her time to move closer to shore without him noticing. *Once again, the hunter becomes the hunted.* Her head was barely above the surface, as her gaze remained locked on his every move. She maneuvered into the shallows, and hid behind emergent plants. The toads frolicked heavily in this area of the pond, and their excessive movement helped obscure Cyndra's presence. In order to get even closer to Daemon, increased stealth was required. She took a deep breath, and completely submerged. Her hands pressed into the sandy bottom as she pulled herself along underwater, following the shoreline toward Daemon. Quietly lifting her head above the surface, she stayed hidden behind foliage.

Daemon stepped slowly on the damp earth close to the water's edge. The dark pond, like a huge cauldron of witch's brew, simmered with its frenzied inhabitants. Lightning sporadically strobed the dismal scene. He couldn't believe he was actually trying to track down and help someone who just tried to kill him. His brush with death was more hellish than he could have imagined, yet it brought him to a powerful new paradigm in his life. He experienced no fear or loathing, but rather acted purposefully in harmony with his heart and mind. A brief drizzly spray refreshed his senses as he kept scanning the water. He trusted his intuitive sense that Cyndra occupied the pond. She felt close by, as if he could feel her breathing.

Like soft breath, something brushed his arm. A sphinx moth buzzed around him. Another began hovering nearby. More and more showed up. They swarmed his face. He swooshed them away, but they kept zooming at him. Their long, wiry tongues reached for his eyes. His achy arms and trembling hands put up a futile defense. Obviously, this swarming of moths was completely unnatural, and more like a directed attack. *Was it from Cyndra? Was it Mara?*

While Daemon brushed and swung at the buzzing swarm, Cyndra slithered through the water along the shore, coming within striking range. Her face contorted as Mara's voice screamed inside her. With Mara's venom in her head, and toxins surging through her body, she was completely wound up and ready to spring into action. When Daemon shouted and flung his arms more frantically, Cyndra lunged at him, clutching her dagger.

A blinding shock wave blasted both of them through the air. Lightning exploded into the water nearby. Daemon collapsed onto the ground, while Cyndra reeled back, and splashed into the pond.

Cyndra floated face down in the water, amid the silent and motionless bodies of aquatic creatures. She awakened to a gentle current, unwinding outward from her suspended form. A silky swirling that grew more ethereal and spacious. An emerging luminosity filled the careening flow, like a spiraling galaxy. Its center fluoresced brightly, and she gravitated toward that sublime light. Immersed in this brilliance, she became more lucid.

Images of her life flared before her. A trembling child mauled by her father, the opiate-based monotone life of her mother, the regime of school faculty constantly testing her, Aunt Lynette, practical and supportive. This flickering panoramic journey shifted and refracted her perception of events. Cast in a new light, even harsh images became more multifaceted and engaging. She rose to a pristine vantage point, discerning significance throughout the expanse of her experiences.

She explored a clashing bouquet of relationships; harmonious, sweet, discordant, foul. A wide spectrum of frequencies that reflected both her outer and inner worlds. Her niche in this ecology of consciousness grew more clear. She flourished with some people, and sequestered the toxicity of others. Everyone and everything traced pathways to either thrive or wither in the terrain of life.

Guided by illuminated curiosity, she drifted into the shadows of this world. Her father's voice echoed around her, yet she maintained a centered focus.

"Cyndra, I'm sorry," his voice humble and

apologetic. Materializing out of the darkness, he grimaced with guilt and sorrow. "You deserved so much better than me for a father."

Cyndra gazed deeply into what had been done to her. She unraveled the web of guilt and shame he had spun. Disentangling from this trap of sticky lies, she realized a more authentic understanding of herself.

His voice trembled. "You are the most beautiful and precious gift I could imagine, yet I poisoned your life."

She felt validated. Her wall of reactive defenses dissolved under a flood of nurturing acceptance. Soothing pearlescent waves delicately rocked her inner child. This soft undulation blurred the edges of her form. Merging into this idyllic current, her renewed spirit infused with her mother and everyone in her life. Washing away soiled memories, she sighed with unblemished beauty. Restored and replenished, she coalesced into a more substantial form. Laughter and tears accompanied the upsurge of euphoric freedom, far beyond her most fantastic dreams.

Mara's tenacious grasp on Cyndra loosened. Her dark presence, like a storm cloud, began to disperse. The rumblings of her destructive commands now silent, Cyndra could hear her own heart song more clearly, and blossomed into a new world of beautiful possibilities.

Visions of Daemon appeared, and his quirky charm and passion for life evoked a warm smile. Drawn to his magnetic eyes and deep soothing voice, she desired his touch. Ecstatic tingles rippled through her, as fantasies of making love to him filled her mind.

However, her passionate indulgence quickly cooled

as Daemon spoke. "Cyndra, it's time for you to leave this place."

"No! I want to stay."

He shook his head and spoke more emphatically. "We must leave now." She felt his arm wrap around her shoulders, nudging her outward. She pushed and resisted leaving this heavenly realm. His pressure became more firm. "We can still be together on the other side."

Cyndra finally acquiesced. Moving away, she grew more heavy and visceral. Like a crystal forming out of solution, she condensed down into her physical frame.

Daemon's hands clenched Cyndra's upper arms and shoulders as he pulled her unmoving body out of the shallows, wondering if it was too late. Without any sign of life, her lithe frame now laid heavy on the earth. Kneeling next to her, one hand over the other, he pumped them powerfully into her chest. Her body shook from the pulsing of his hands. He strove to go deep enough to be effective, and hoped her ribs would not crack in the process. His heart beat powerfully for Cyndra to live. It pounded his whole body, throbbing through his arms and hands, and into Cyndra's chest. He fought for her life like it was his own. Sweat gathered on his face. Countless precious moments went by. It began to feel hopeless. "Come on Cyndra, breathe!"

As if hearing his voice, her mouth opened with an audible gasp. Her chest and belly filled with air, she arched up, then slumped down. She coughed a few times then became quiet and still. The slow rise and fall of breath incrementally drew her back to this world.

Daemon had no idea of how much time had passed. He clasped his hands around hers and waited. Relieved she is alive, yet his brow furrowed wondering what she will be like coming back.

Cyndra's head quivered. She opened her eyes, pale and glistening, no longer black. Her lips opened again, a faint, raspy voice emerged. "Where am I?"

The devilish spell she had been under seemed to be broken. Daemon leaned in. "You're safe, here in the garden." One hand embraced her shoulder, the other was held at his heart.

Cyndra's eyes looked far away. She cleared her throat, and spoke in garbled tones. "It was so beautiful...why did you bring me back?"

A brief look of surprise was followed by a more serious expression of understanding. *She must have had an altered state of consciousness, probably a near death experience.* After a moment he answered, "You brought me to a world beyond all dreams. I want to share that world with you."

Cyndra whispered, "I remember a terrible nightmare." She swallowed as a confused look came over her face. "Or...was it *just* a dream?" Her eyes apprehensively waited for the answer.

"It's all over now," he said reassuringly, "time to rest." Although trying to alleviate her fears, he indirectly affirmed them as well. His hands again gently cradled and warmed hers. "It's okay. It wasn't your fault... it wasn't even *you*." His head shook slowly. "It was Mara; it was mind control."

Cyndra's face reddened and her eyes flooded with

227

tears from the crushing realization of what she had done. Her body heaved with anguish. Quivering lips uttered, "I'm so sorry," as she curled into a fetal position.

Daemon's heart expanded with compassion; for her, for himself, and for anyone who had been deeply hurt by such horrible forces. "You're alive and safe, that's all that matters," he said, gently stroking her wet hair. After a while, he helped prop her up to sitting. Daemon nestled close with his arms around her, keeping her warm. Clouds receded from the moon, and they drew even closer in that strong magnetic light. With a snug hold, they anchored each other back into this world.

"Can you stand up?" he asked. "I can help you walk."

Cyndra nodded as they grabbed each other's arms. With firm yet gentle traction Daemon pulled her to an upright position.

He braced her firmly next to him, as they hobbled back to her house. The same path he had hurried through in dread not too long ago. "You'll be cleaned up and in dry clothes before you know it." On the journey back, Daemon kept reassuring her everything was going to be okay, although he wondered how she would recover from all this trauma. As they arrived at the guest house, there was a rustling in the bushes.

Daemon stopped. "Be careful Cyndra, let me see what it is." He leaned over and parted some low branches. A dark form moved toward him. It meowed

Cyndra's face lit up and gasped, "Nisha, you're alive!" She staggered closer. Leaning down, her hands slid around its sleek coat and picked her up. She hugged the reclaimed cat tightly as it purred. Cyndra's injured body managed to gently sway with the love of her pet. "But if you're alive, who did I bury?" she asked, looking over at the mound of wilting leaves and flowers.

Daemon dug through the pile, uncovering what Cyndra had mistaken for her cat. It was an artificial but quite realistic copy of Nisha. So detailed and precise, he immediately thought of the person with the expendable resources for such a thing, Mara. As they stepped back to the path leading to Cyndra's house, Daemon spotted a greeting card laying on the ground. Lifting and opening it up, he realized there was not enough light to read, and so stashed it in his pocket. While Cyndra continued to support her soft friend, Daemon's arm wrapped around her and guided them both inside the house.

He handed her a bottled water and draped a towel over her shoulders. "Ready for a shower?" he asked. She nodded as he helped her over to the bathroom. "I've got a few things to do. Meet me back at the lab when you're ready."

As he prepared to leave, he grabbed her phone. He also remembered the note in his pocket and pulled it out into the light.

In honor of your little friend, I hope to secure the link between us.
Mara.

It confirmed his suspicions, but also raised questions. *What was this for? What was Mara up to?* He exited, making sure the door was locked securely behind him.

In El Dorado Village, many homes sat quietly in darkness, but not the Blackstone residence. With generators banging out excessive power, Mara's fortress gleamed arrogantly on the outside, yet suffered severe short circuits inside. The door to the mind manipulation room was ajar, and the scent of burned machinery hung in the air. Romantic music continued playing against the background of the engines of electricity. The psychotronic screen flashed, *SYSTEM OVERLOAD-RESET.* Mara's body lay sprawled out on the floor, amid spilled champagne and broken glass. Still hooked up to her vital signs monitor, it registered a flat line. Her lifeless eyes were half open, and hair scorched, from the blowback of energy through her system. Cyndra's electrocution had blasted an energy overload through the mind warping technology, leaving Mara a victim of her own shadow. After all her planning on vortex energy, she had acquired an unexpected portal. The portal of death.

Moving steadily through dark, mushy pathways, Daemon returned to the scene of his paralysis. For a moment, his face cringed with the thoughts and feelings of that horrific experience. Determined to let go of that event, he continued to act deliberately. Using Cyndra's phone, he dialed his number and found his phone. He ventured to the lab, where he turned on some battery powered lamps. Looking at the many bottles of extracts, he instinctively knew what to mix. Everything appeared more clear and information rich. He carefully poured one elixir after another into a drinking glass, until a dozen opened bottles sat next to it. Into this he drizzled various honeys and a touch of fulvic acid. He stirred it and took a few gulps of the bitter sweet liquid.

Unexpectedly, the overhead lights popped back on. The lab equipment buzzed and whirred with the return of power. Despite this, he couldn't get online with his computer. The modem was not working; the cord was missing. Noticing a cabinet door not completely shut, he found the cord and immediately hooked it up. Emailing El Dorado Village, he expressed a willingness to move ahead fairly, with healthy boundaries. Messaging Caloosa University, he apologized, and expressed plans to improve communication and accountability. He called Lynette to make sure she arrived promptly, yet without upsetting her.

"Hi Lynette, sorry to be calling at this hour," said Daemon.

"That's okay, I was just getting ready for my early flight back. How's Cyndra? asked Lynette. "Is everything alright?"

"Well, she was stung by bees earlier, but she seems okay."

"Those are killer bees. Did you take her to a hospital?"

"No, even though it was a shock to her system, she's recovering quite well."

"Are you sure? It sounds awful."

"See for yourself when you get here. Just thought I'd give you a head's up. I'll fill you in on all the details later."

"Okay. Keep an eye on her and I'll be there around

noon."

The moon was sinking behind the trees; it would soon be dawn. The longest day of the year, and of Daemon's life, was finally coming to an end. He reflected on the powerful journey he had been on since Cyndra's arrival. Taking the Utopia Nectar simply reaffirmed who he had now become, although it added a deeply restorative effect.

Cyndra entered the lab, clean, warm and dry. Easing herself onto a seat next to Daemon, they looked at each other and smiled.

"Try this," he said, handing her the nectar.

She drank it, and crinkled her nose. "Needs more honey," she said with a cough.

"Maybe for you; I'm cutting back," he said with a wink.

Her eyes sparkled more than he had seen in many days. She snuggled closer, and laid her head on his shoulder. Her breath warmed his heart. He felt more strongly for her than anyone or anything in his life. They sat together, for a brief eternity, communing silently in the twilight of the new day. At last, Daemon's voice broke the stillness.

"Cyndra, I want nothing more than to be with you. To share our lives together."

Her eyes shimmered like the Caribbean Sea. "I've wanted you since we first met." She tilted her head. "But just be careful what you ask for."

"What do you mean?"

"I don't think there's any antidote for the spell *you've*

put me under."

Daemon's warm chocolate eyes held Cyndra's bright blue gaze, like the attraction between earth and sky. Their intimacy spawned a precious state of wonder; a portal into a new life. They drew closer. Her soft breath caressed his face. His lips tenderly pressed onto hers in a delicious embrace, nurturing the utopia of deep surrender into oneness. Sunrise filled the room with golden light, and transcendent illumination infused a garden blossoming with dreams of love.

Made in the USA
Las Vegas, NV
03 December 2021